# THE LEFT HAND
# OF JUSTICE

# What Reviewers Say About Jess Faraday's Work

"*The Affair of the Porcelain Dog* is an excellent mystery. The characters are complex and in general not what they seem on first sight. Many unexpected twists and turns keep the novel intriguing right up to the end."—*Gay, Lesbian, Bisexual, and Transgender Round Table of the American Library Association*

"*The Affair of the Porcelain Dog* is a thoughtful book, a well-put-together mystery that integrates relationship problems into the main framework, but it is also an action-packed book...If you are a fan of Victorian-era mystery, or of strong LGBT characters in a story that does not rely on sex to move the plot along, *Porcelain Dog* is an excellent pick for your next read."—Anthony Cardno, *Chelsea Street Station No. 1*

"Jess Faraday takes you into a very bleak, dangerous, and inhuman realm. A world without mercy. But despite all this, she's able to deliver a beautiful and romantic story. ...This clever multi-layered mystery skillfully combined with some very strong characters will definitely keep you in suspense until the very end."—*Booked Up Reviews*

"Whether you like detective fiction, noir, Victorian stories or just damned good love stories, this will appeal to you."—*Erastes, Speak Its Name Reviews*

"The author builds a credible plot through the actions of diverse, fully-nuanced characters, which keeps the reader interested... Excellent first novel by a promising new author, which I give five stars out of five."—Bob Lind, *Echo Magazine*

"...despite all the ugliness it dealt with it managed to be also sweet and romantic..."—*Elisa Reviews*

Visit us at www.boldstrokesbooks.com

## By the Author

# THE LEFT HAND
# OF JUSTICE

*by*

Jess Faraday

2013

# THE LEFT HAND OF JUSTICE

ISBN 10: 1-60282-863-6
ISBN 13: 978-1-60282-863-6

THIS TRADE PAPERBACK ORIGINAL IS PUBLISHED BY
BOLD STROKES BOOKS, INC.
P.O. BOX 249
VALLEY FALLS, NY 12185

FIRST EDITION: MARCH 2013

---

CREDITS
EDITORS: GREG HERREN & SHELLEY THRASHER
PRODUCTION DESIGN: SUSAN RAMUNDO
COVER DESIGN BY SHERI (GRAPHICARTIST2020@HOTMAIL.COM)

# Acknowledgments

Merci beaucoup to both of my writing groups—PCG and the Book 'Em Writing Group—whose insights made this book shine. Thanks also to Jean Utley of Book 'Em Mystery Bookstore in South Pasadena, CA, for her generosity and unflagging championing of local and fledgling authors. Greatest thanks, as ever, are reserved for my long-suffering Roy, without whose support and encouragement not a word would ever have been written.

# CHAPTER ONE

I nspector!"
The little boy's voice at her door pulled Inspector Elise Corbeau back from warm, dreamless sleep—back into the biting bone-chill of the Paris night. The boy, Joseph, was her eyes and ears in the slums of the Montagne Ste. Geneviève. When things went bump in the night, he was the one who came to fetch her.

And since the new chief inspector had shut down the Bureau of Supernatural Investigations, a lot of things had been going bump.

"Inspector, open up!"

"It's still dark," she muttered, throwing off the covers. Her head was thick with sleep. But at least she'd slept a good few hours, and at least the night had sent Joseph and not another of Ugly Jacques's men.

Joseph began to batter the door with the end of his wooden leg.

"Peace, child. I'm coming."

Corbeau reached for the lamp on the wobbly bedside table and gave it a shake. Finding it nearly empty, she set it back down without lighting it. Her room was as spare as a monk's and less than eight long paces across. She'd save the oil for when she really needed it.

Gingerly, she pulled herself upright, cradling her head in her hands. Her skull felt like an eggshell. A woolen dress lay crumpled at the foot of the bed. She pulled it over her nightshirt and cinched a thick leather belt around her waist. Then she slid the strap of a rectangular bag over her head and one shoulder. It contained the tools issued to every Bureau agent: bottles of iron filings, holy water, and salt—the dearest of the three and the lowest in supply. The bag also contained a rosary and a small, fat book of prayers in Latin, Greek, and Hebrew. She pulled a box from under the bed and added half a dozen of the pills she had compounded the week before. The original recipe, a mild sedative, had come from her mother, a healer. Over time Corbeau had used her own knowledge and experience to refine it into an invaluable tool for subduing the natural and supernatural alike.

She tied back her stringy blond hair and stretched her neck and shoulders. Her left arm ached where Ugly Jacques's collector had tried to separate it from her body earlier that night. With any luck, the next one wouldn't find her before she received her miserable pay at the beginning of the month. But just in case, she pulled her truncheon from its place between the bed and the wall and tucked it into her belt as well.

She dragged herself across cold, bare wood to the door. Rattling open the locks, she blinked down at Joseph through bleary eyes. The darkness was so deep she could only make out the edges of his shape. But she didn't need flickering paraffin light to know what she would see: a pinched, white face with light-brown eyes, brown hair the texture of straw sticking out from under a brown cloth cap, and some other child's cast-off clothes hanging like rags from his birdlike limbs. As he shifted from side to side, she heard the unmistakable squeak of new boot-leather. Who had bought him shoes?

"Another one?" she asked, pushing back a yawn.

"'Fraid so, Inspector."

"That makes three, then."

Three supernatural disturbances in the slum that week. Michel Bertrand was the first—a stout young man with the whiff of the stables about him, half-insane from nightmares he insisted were coming true. Then there was Claudine Fournier, a surprisingly refined young woman, given the broken-down rooming house where

Corbeau had found her. Mademoiselle Fournier, too, was troubled by nightmares—only her nightmares were manifesting themselves in this world through spontaneous fires and glass objects bursting from no other cause than Mademoiselle looking at them. Corbeau had subdued the nightmares but left with singed hair and fingertips. Corbeau had managed to settle Bertrand and Fournier before the gossipmongers who made their living selling rumors to the scandal sheets had caught wind of them, but if things kept going like this, it would only be a matter of time before they did.

During her tenure with the now-defunct Bureau of Supernatural Investigations—before the new chief inspector had demoted her to fetching coffee and filing papers—Detective Inspector Elise Corbeau had answered such calls as a matter of course. Only a handful of incidents had necessitated actual spiritual intervention. But the recent incidents were different. Corbeau hadn't been able to trace these disturbances to whistling wind or seeping damp. And she no longer had the support of the Bureau, her fellow agents, or their leader and mentor, Eugène Vidocq.

The floorboards felt like ice beneath her feet. Corbeau glanced longingly back at her narrow bed piled high with covers rapidly losing their warmth.

"It's in our building this time," Joseph said, sensing her hesitation. Ugly Jacques wasn't the only one Corbeau owed. Joseph's mother would be sending for Corbeau every time something went bump in her night for the rest of her life.

And Corbeau would have to drop everything and go.

Corbeau sighed. "Let me get my coat."

She pulled on stockings, laced up her boots, and ushered the boy back into the tight blackness of the hallway. She buttoned her coat as they felt their way down the hall. She had candle stubs and a tinderbox in her pocket, but she wouldn't squander them on the stairwell that she knew better in darkness than in daylight. Seconds later she and Joseph had wound their way down three cramped and creaky flights of stairs and stood shivering on the street in the weak light of an unreliably maintained streetlamp.

"Hard night?" Joseph asked.

"Hmm? Oh." Her hand went to her face, fingers probing the tender, swelling cheek that throbbed in the early November chill. No doubt the skin was already turning an impressive shade of purple. "Something like that."

"Ugly Jacques?"

She threw him a rueful glance. No nine-year-old should know the name of Paris's most notorious moneylender. Less still should he know about Corbeau's own financial difficulties. The Saint Christopher medal she'd given him glinted from the band of his cap.

"A little excessive for two weeks' pay," she muttered, abandoning the pretense of protecting him. "Of course the way prices are rising, he probably wants to get his money while it's still worth something."

"I bet you taught his man a lesson, though," Joseph said with a smirk.

Corbeau grinned, and winced as pain shot through her head. She had left the bastard unconscious on the floor of Oubliette in a pool of broken glass and cheap wine. It had been a shameful waste of wine.

"Don't suppose you've got cab fare, then," Joseph said.

Corbeau's eyes went to his wooden leg. She didn't know how he'd gotten to her building, but he probably couldn't walk all the way back home. Although he certainly seemed sprightly that night. She looked again.

"Where's your crutch?"

Joseph usually limped along on a wooden post strapped to his leg just below the knee. Having had the apparatus since he was six, he'd become adept enough to become a useful messenger, provided he could catch a ride now and then. Without the crutch, though, he had a slow, lurching gait, like a drunkard.

But just now he'd scrambled down the stairs in front of her, unassisted and as nimble as a goat. She peered closer at his new boots. Two of them.

"You've got a foot under there," Corbeau said.

He grinned. "A proper one, with hinges on the ankle and toes."

"You steal it?"

"Naw," he said, with mock offense. "It was payment for a job well done. The shoes, too."

"What kind of job?"

"Now, Inspector, how could I get the kind of work that pays in shoes if I went around running my mouth to the police?"

She narrowed her eyes.

"We'll talk about this later."

He followed her long strides down the street, around the corner into an alley, where a man was snoring under a blanket on the front bench of an open cart. She'd thought to let Victor go home to his wife when he'd dropped her off earlier, but a little voice had told her she'd need him later. She was glad she'd listened. Corbeau laid her hand over the nose of the sturdy piebald harnessed to the front of the cart and whispered a few words of encouragement before giving the wheel a kick.

"Up, Victor!" she said sharply. "We've work to do!"

She wasn't the only one in Paris who owed someone a favor. From the man's grumbling, Corbeau guessed he was probably wishing he'd sold the blasted horse to the knacker. The animal hadn't been possessed, as Victor had thought, but lack of it would have relieved him of the ability to take Corbeau around at all hours. And he wouldn't owe her for having settled the matter.

"Where to now, Inspector?" he grunted after Corbeau and Joseph had settled themselves on the thin covering of straw in the cart bed.

"Montagne Ste. Geneviève," Joseph said.

Victor turned around gruffly at the impertinent little voice. A sudden clap of thunder shook the air.

"As the boy says."

"All right, then," Victor said. "Let's get this over with."

## CHAPTER TWO

Half an hour later, Victor's cart skidded to a stop on the slick cobblestones before Joseph's building, a tumbledown rooming house owned by his mother, the widow Bernard. A fat droplet of rain burst on Corbeau's cheek as the widow stepped out of the shadows of the front door to meet them.

"Thank you for coming, Inspector," she said, holding up a sputtering candle as Corbeau swung her leg over the side of the cart.

A sudden crash shook the house behind them. Victor's horse started, and Corbeau barely had time to lift Joseph clear before the animal dashed off down the road, the cart careering wildly in its wake.

Gripping Joseph firmly by the hand, Corbeau followed the widow through the small crowd that had gathered. Women huddled beneath moth-eaten blankets. Sleepy-eyed men stamped feet rag-wrapped against the cold. Despite the hour, the cutting chill, and the tingle of the impending downpour in the air, their expressions made it clear that they'd rather take their chances on the dark, dirty street than inside.

"What is it, Inspector?" someone asked. Another cold drip fell on Corbeau's face.

"A noisy spirit?"

"The devil himself?"

Corbeau kept walking. If she stopped to explain her theory—and that she'd seldom encountered either spirits or demons in her many, many years of investigating these kinds of disturbances—she'd be there arguing with them all night while some poor soul suffered.

Inside, the rooming house was all peeling paint and dark corners, the air thick with the mingled odors of sweat and burning coal. It was no palace, but thanks to Corbeau's continued payments, the widow was close to owning it outright. Joseph's mother might work until her fingers bled, but she and her children would never starve. That had to be worth something—perhaps even the right foot of a six-year-old boy.

As they crept up the stairs, Joseph clumping along at their heels, Madame Bernard's tallow candle guttered and spat, emitting more black smoke than light. The widow was probably about Corbeau's age, approaching thirty, with similar traces of early responsibility etched around her mouth and eyes, and a sprinkling of gray in her dark hair. Her thin build hid a stout heart; she hadn't summoned Corbeau lightly—which made Corbeau even more wary of what she would find.

Suspicion prickled up Corbeau's spine as they ascended the stairs together. When the air around them began to vibrate, Corbeau stopped. The sound was so low that probably only her trained ear recognized it as sound; others would sense only an inexplicable feeling of menace. It was a sensation Corbeau would always associate with the one true demonic possession she had witnessed. That had been her first year with the Bureau—long enough in the past that most days she could pretend she'd imagined the whole thing. But at times like this, she realized the terror of that day was permanently etched onto her heart.

"Has this been going on long?" she asked.

"An hour, maybe two."

"Am I the only one you called?"

"Yes, Inspector."

"No priests?"

"No, Inspector. No police, either. Only you."

Given the one-time competition between Bureau agents and His Holiness's exorcists, and the uncomfortably close relationship His Majesty was forging with the Church, the last thing Corbeau wanted to encounter at the scene was a priest. Except, perhaps, for a fellow Sûreté agent. Though intervention from the prefect's office had kept Vautrin from sacking her with the rest of her colleagues, Corbeau wasn't at all certain her benefactor would continue to protect her if she was discovered violating the chief inspector's order to leave supernatural matters to the Church.

On the second-floor landing, the widow Bernard paused to pull her shawl tighter around her shoulders. Corbeau rubbed her hands together. The temperature had dropped noticeably between the ground and second floors. Shivering—and not entirely from the chill—she laid a hand on her truncheon and followed Madame Bernard to a door at the end of the hall.

"Right here, number four."

Corbeau tensed as something crashed against the door. She swallowed.

"When you're ready," she said.

With a determined nod, the widow chose a key from the ring chained to the waistband of her skirt.

The air inside the apartment thrummed with the menace Corbeau had felt in the stairwell, only here it was strong enough to rattle their bones. Objects—a tin cup, a chamber pot, a Bible—floated through the air, describing wobbly orbits around the room's perimeter. No wind had been blowing when Corbeau arrived, but on the opposite wall, grimy curtains whipped in and out of an open window. A shirtless, sweating man stood at the center of the chaos. He was younger than Corbeau, but tall and athletically formed, with curly dark hair recently trimmed and thick, dark chin stubble. His large, dark eyes twitched toward them, then rolled back into his skull as he shuddered violently.

The hair stood up on Corbeau's arms—an irrational response. She had to get ahold of herself. *Nothing more than an atavistic fear of insanity shared by peoples across time and space.* That's what Vidocq had taught them, and in most cases, it was enough to put panic in its place. To Corbeau's experience, undiscovered spiritual talents were often at the root of the disturbances the academically minded described as insanity, and which the superstitious interpreted as demonic possession.

Still, it paid to be cautious.

"Bell, book, and candle, if you please, Madame," she said, without looking away. "And take your son with you."

The widow Bernard didn't question why a police inspector was asking for a priest's tools. She simply seemed happy to be dismissed. Normally, that would have been the point. Familiar-sounding objects and rites comforted the superstitious and kept them out of the way. In the past, people had been more comfortable thinking there was a demoniac in their midst—an evil they already believed in and could understand—than hearing about uncontrolled spiritual energies erupting from unsuspecting individuals. But with the waves of religious hysteria traveling through the areas recently, would that continue to be the case?

"Hello," Corbeau called. The man's head jerked toward her. His upper lip curled, and he let out a low, rumbling snarl like a dog. Corbeau sucked in her breath and straightened. "That's enough. You can stop now."

He did. She let out a long, tense breath. Six times out of seven, an outburst of spiritual energies could be halted simply by informing the perpetrator the energies were part of him. But first, one had to command the subject's attention—not an easy thing when the subject was using his mind to toss the place. Corbeau took a step forward. The tin cup flew out of its orbit and whizzed toward her face. Corbeau lifted her truncheon the second before the cup hit her forehead. It glanced harmlessly off the baton and floated back toward the edge of the room.

"This isn't what you think it is," she said, raising her voice above the feral noises vibrating in the walls and floorboards. "You're not under attack by the Evil One or anyone else, though it probably feels like it." A chamber pot hurtled toward her. Corbeau ducked, and it crashed against the doorjamb, spattering the walls with dark urine. A candle end flew at her next, then a shoe. "I can help you if you let me. But you have to stop throwing things."

The man cocked his head. The animal noises stopped. Corbeau felt some of the tension in her shoulders release. Was it really going to be this easy? The last two incidents hadn't been. She had gone through all the standard steps, and when those hadn't worked, she'd sprinkled some holy water, recited a few prayers in Latin, and given the perpetrators a couple of the white pills from her bag. She'd left them both asleep in their beds, not knowing whether she'd actually solved anything.

But no one had summoned her back.

"That's right," she continued. She wiped one palm on her coat and crept closer. "You're doing this. And if you want me to help, you have to control yourself. What's your name?"

The man's breathing quickened. His eyes rolled back in his head and he began to shiver. Just like the others, and unlike anything she'd encountered with the Bureau. Yet there was something familiar about these incidents. Something about them echoed long-ago memories Corbeau had worked hard to forget. Memories from a different time, a different life, when she had gone by another name and Sûreté agent Elise Corbeau had yet to come into existence.

She shook her head. *Impossible*, she scolded herself. That was nearly a decade in the past, and she'd covered her tracks twice over.

Corbeau swallowed again. The baton was slippery in her hand. She fingered open the buckles of the bag at her waist. If this was an outburst of latent spiritual energies, the procedures Vidocq had taught them should suffice. All the same, she slipped her hand inside, unstoppered the bottle of holy water, and wet her fingers just in case. Keeping the truncheon between the man and herself, she touched a wet fingertip to the middle of his forehead and two others above his eyebrows. His skin was hot and damp, but he didn't jerk away from the holy water. *No demon, then*, she noted with relief. His eyes closed and the trembling decreased. She let out a long breath.

"What's your name?" she asked again.

"Lambert. Armand Lambert."

"Monsieur Lambert, I'm Detective Inspector Elise Corbeau. You're experiencing a spiritual disturbance of your own making. It's frightening, but you can control it. Do you understand?" She coaxed a pill from the pillbox in her bag. "Here. Take this." He placed it on the back of his tongue and swallowed. "Breathe deeply. Don't open your eyes until I tell you to."

Lambert squeezed his eyes shut tighter and drew a shaking breath. Corbeau removed her hand from his forehead and collected her thoughts. From her experience, this sort of outburst was most common in highly strung adolescent girls. But the two recent cases had been adults: one man and one woman. The incidents had also taken place in the slums of the Montagne Ste. Geneviève, just a brisk walk from this very building.

She could remember similar disturbances clustering in a single area only one other time. The disturbances had had nothing to do with demons. Rather, they had been caused by greed—people's greed to develop supernatural talents they did not necessarily possess, and the greed of Moreau the Alchemist for their money. By the time the Sûreté founder Vidocq had kicked down her laboratory door, her concoctions had driven many to the madhouse or the grave. Guilt and panic crept up her throat once more. She pushed them down.

This was different. It had to be. She had destroyed her laboratory, her store of ingredients, and her notes. At Vidocq's side, she had dismantled the networks of people who had distributed her potions and tinctures; every last one was in prison or dead. And when her debt to society had been paid in full, Vidocq had erased all traces of Moreau the Alchemist, and Elise Corbeau, Agent of the Sûreté, had been born.

That was over with. Done. These new incidents could not possibly be related.

This was not her fault.

She returned her attention to the young man in the center of the room. He had released some of the tension in his shoulders and was starting to shiver.

Like the other victims, Armand Lambert was an adult. He spoke in a city dweller's clipped staccato; he hadn't come in from the country to work the factories like his neighbors had. His hands were smooth and unstained, and his tidy brown curls suggested he was used to keeping himself well groomed. A servant, perhaps. A clerk or shop assistant. No longer employed, judging by the three-day stubble on his chin. Like the other victims, his possessions were minimal. Corbeau opened the wardrobe. He was wearing his only set of clothing.

Like the other victims, Armand Lambert was running from something.

"How are you feeling now, Mr. Lambert?" Corbeau asked. Lambert blinked and opened his eyes. He looked better, more in control. He was breathing easier. Unlike with the last two victims, she might actually get some information out of him. One by one, his possessions began to drop out of their orbits, falling harmlessly on the bed, the chair, and the floor. "Has this happened before?" Lambert nodded. Corbeau felt a pang of sympathy. It must have been terrifying for him. Had he thought himself haunted? "Some people think that everyone has untapped spiritual powers— powers that are only waiting for something to trigger them. Have you experienced any sort of major upset in your life recently? The death of a loved one, for example?"

Lambert shook his head. Corbeau frowned. Spiritual energies rarely erupted without provocation, in her experience. It would have been comforting to believe that this was one of those rare occasions, but that left the other two, which had not only occurred within the same geographical area, but within the same week.

Corbeau handed him the shirt from the wardrobe, and he meekly shrugged it over his shoulders. He looked up at her as if to say something, but before he could, footsteps thundered up the stairs. Madame Bernard and Joseph, Corbeau guessed from the familiar sound of their footfall. But they weren't alone.

"Inspector—" Madame Bernard said, bursting into the room. A man rushed in on her heels—a tall, angular man with fiery eyes and an important manner. He wore an expensive coat and boots, and his white collar peeked out from beneath his pointed chin.

"I thought you said you didn't call for a priest!" Corbeau cried.

"The Lord summoned me."

The priest was younger than Corbeau and looked eager to prove himself. *To whom,* she wondered. *And how had he known to come?* Corbeau's heart raced. If this got back to the chief inspector, she'd be out on her ear without a hearing. The priest didn't look like the sort who would suffer an interloper. His nails were clean, his robes crisp, and he was cracking his knuckles in anticipation of a fight. With the devil or with her, it wouldn't matter.

"It was thoughtful of Him," Corbeau said carefully, "but unnecessary. Monsieur Lambert was having a nightmare, nothing more." She breathed a sigh of relief that all signs of the extraordinary had dissipated. In the doorway, one-footed Joseph smirked. She turned to the widow Bernard. "You can tell the others that it's safe to return. Monsieur Lambert has finished throwing his things around."

Lambert looked sheepish. The priest looked irate. Corbeau glanced around the room again. She might have solved Lambert's problem—for now—but it wouldn't be the last incident—not until she figured out what was triggering them. And now that the Church was involved, she would have to find a way to work around both it and the new chief inspector. Another set of footsteps coming up the stairs shook her from her thoughts. When Vautrin himself entered the room, her heart sank.

"I came as quickly as I could, Father."

Unlike the priest, the new chief inspector had seen his share of action. It showed on his weathered face and in the hard layer of muscles that lay under the softer layer he had acquired as growing administrative duties had overtaken street-level police work. His dark eyes were cruel, and, more often than not, he appeared as if he'd just stepped in something unpleasant.

"Why?" Corbeau asked. A mistake, but she couldn't help herself. Vautrin had closed down the Bureau of Supernatural Investigations, saying that such incidents were the purview of the Church, not the police. And yet here he was. With the priest.

The chief inspector looked around, his eyes narrowing as they fixed on her. Another set of footsteps reached the landing, and a third man joined them—young, inexperienced, and pressing his thin frame against the wall as if it would keep any ghosts from seeing him. One of Vautrin's new hires, then. At most, a month's experience on the streets, and less than none dealing with the supernatural. The three men edged her out of the way, surrounded Lambert, and began some sort of inspection.

"Chief Inspector, you have no—"

Vautrin turned to her, his voice a sharp-edged knife. "I didn't expect to see you here, Madame." He refused to call her Inspector. He had refused from the moment they had been introduced. The Bureau of Supernatural Investigations had offended Vautrin's religious sensibilities. The presence of a female agent offended him on all levels. The prefect might not have allowed Vautrin to dismiss Corbeau outright, but Vautrin was doing his level best to make her wish that he had. "You have no business here," Vautrin said. "The Bureau no longer exists, and you've been relieved of your investigative duties."

"The owner of the property requested my presence," said Corbeau.

Madame Bernard straightened, lifted her chin, and fixed Vautrin with a defiant gaze.

"That very well may be. But demonic possession is a matter for the Church."

"There are no demons here," Corbeau said, as Vautrin's man laid hold of Lambert and shoved him up against the wall. Getting nowhere with Vautrin, she approached the priest. "He didn't react to holy water, and—" She turned back to Vautrin. "Even if there were a demon, Chief Inspector, you said yourself that the Sûreté has no business—"

Anger flashed in Vautrin's deep-set eyes. His square jaw clenched and he drew a sharp breath. "His Majesty desires the police to take a greater role in guarding public morality, and I intend to follow through on this desire, whether Claude Javert agrees or not." He spat out the name as if it tasted foul.

Corbeau's ears pricked up. Claude Javert, the prefect of police, had come to his position straight from the Jesuits. Well known for his efficiency and uncompromising logic, Javert and the zealot Vautrin should see eye to eye on His Majesty's moral crusade. Could it be that they did not? Corbeau wanted to ask, but the dangerous light in Vautrin's face warned her off. "How does a nightmare violate public morality?" she asked instead.

He glared at her for a moment longer, then turned to the priest. "Well, Father, what's your opinion?"

"Mmm?"

The priest gave a grunt and a nod. Vautrin's man unbuttoned Lambert's shirt. The sedative she had given him was beginning to take effect. He looked at the priest, confused, as the priest lifted his arm. Something glittered near the thatch of dark hair beneath the arm—something metal, something golden—that appeared to be part of the skin itself.

"What on Earth—" Corbeau began to say.

"The devil's mark," said the priest, shoving Lambert's arm away in disgust.

"That's rubbish! There's metal under there, grafted right into the skin." Corbeau stepped forward, but without warning, Vautrin sprang at her, pushing her back with the strength of a runaway draft horse. They slammed into the wall, Vautrin pinning her to the wall by her neck with his truncheon. "Let go of him!" she cried again.

"You have no authority here, Madame," he hissed, his thin lips just inches from her chin.

"By your own definition, neither do you."

"God's authority is behind me."

"Then why didn't He tell you about the other two incidents?"

Vautrin's face paled. Corbeau felt a rush of triumph. He hadn't known about Bertrand and Fournier. And, from the way his lips were pursing themselves bloodless, she could see that he desperately wanted to have known. He probably considered it his sacred duty. His hands tightened around the ends of the baton, making it tremble on her windpipe. It was clear how badly he wanted to push it all the way to the wall.

"What now, Chief Inspector?" The young officer's question probably saved Corbeau's life. Vautrin turned. The truncheon eased away from Corbeau's throat, but he stayed in front of her, blocking her way.

"Take him down to the wagon."

"But—" Corbeau said

Vautrin's face whipped back toward her, and he slammed the baton up below her chin. Grasping Lambert by the arms, the priest and the young officer moved him forward. Lambert stumbled, his limbs now clumsy and leaden from the sedative. A different kind of guilt balled up in Corbeau's stomach. She might not have caused Lambert's outburst with her clumsy medicine, but she had enabled Vautrin and the priest to take him away without a fight. Out of the corner of her eye, she saw something glint in the lamplight on the floor near the bed.

"You may have friends in high places, Madame," Vautrin growled so low that she was the only one who could hear him, "but breathe a word of this to anyone, and I'll slit your throat myself."

He gave the baton a final push before tucking it back into his belt and pulling his coat around him. Madame Bernard held Joseph close as Vautrin swept out of the room after the priest. When their footsteps had safely reached the bottom of the stairs, Corbeau slumped against the wall, rubbing her throat.

"Inspector?" Joseph asked after a moment.

"There," she said hoarsely. "By the foot of the bed. Made of glass. Bring it here."

Pulling free of his mother, Joseph crossed the room and retrieved the object, a small phial. Corbeau turned it over in her fingers. A drop of clear liquid slid from one end to the other. She sniffed at the opening, jerking back at the sudden onslaught of familiar scents: valerian, mugwort, poppy, and a few other things she couldn't identify. It was a strange combination—not one that a ghetto healer would think to put together.

But something an alchemist would.

"What is it, Inspector?" Madame Bernard asked.

Corbeau's heart pounded. Her cheeks went hot, and as she turned to this woman to whom her debt would never be extinguished, the weight of her guilt was a crushing band around her chest. Another alchemist was working the streets of Paris, and it appeared they were building on her work—work she thought she'd destroyed all evidence of nearly a decade before.

"Inspector?"

It couldn't be. She sniffed the phial again, but she had made no mistake. On the night of her arrest those many years ago, Corbeau had consigned her books and notes to the fire. She had taken a chair to her distillery. Nothing remained of her past, and those who remembered her as the Alchemist were few, far between, and not available for consultation.

And yet someone was producing her elixirs again. Or attempting to. And Vidocq was long gone.

"Excuse me, Madame," Corbeau muttered.

She stuffed the phial into her coat pocket, brushing past Madame Bernard and her son in her rush for the stairs. Outside on the street, she forced herself to draw deep, steadying breaths of the freezing night air.

## CHAPTER THREE

Corbeau pushed through the dispersing crowd, the bottle clenched tightly in her hand. The hard November wind whipped at her hems. She shoved her hands into her coat pockets as rain pelted her cheeks. People were going to die. Go mad and die. She might not have compounded the new formulae herself, but whoever had, was using her work as a foundation. Worse than that, Vautrin had his nasty fingers in it already.

And then there was the Church.

A crack of thunder shook the air. Lightning lit the street like daylight before plunging it back into darkness.

"Detective!" A woman's voice cut through the storm. The gossipmongers were the only ones who called her Detective anymore—those low, skulking creatures always sniffing around for a tidbit to sell to the newspapers. It figured they would find her when the only information she had would incriminate her. She kept walking. "Detective!"

"If you want a story, talk to the chief inspector."

The wind stretched out her words, chopped them up. It'd be interesting to see how the chief inspector would tell it, though it would never happen. As much as the man liked to see his name in print, whatever he had planned for Lambert wasn't going to make the papers. It wouldn't even appear in the internal documents that Corbeau would be expected to file.

She walked faster, but it only seemed to make the other woman more determined. Corbeau smirked as she heard high heels *clip-clop* over the cobblestones behind her. The woman had better watch out. One didn't want to turn an ankle in this neighborhood.

"Bernadette!" the woman shouted.

Corbeau stopped. Bernadette Moreau—she hadn't used that name since Vidocq had inducted her into the Sûreté. Turning, she exhaled with a mixture of relief and exasperation as she recognized the figure tottering out of the gloom toward her, darting around broken pavement and black puddles. "I told you never to call me that, Sophie."

"You've been avoiding me for a month." The woman pouted as she took Corbeau's arm and began to pull her along. "I've missed you." Her dress, coat, and reddish-blond hair were immaculate despite the hour. A cat-and-canary smile flickered at the edges of her painted lips. She might sell information to every leftist publication in Paris, but apparently it didn't mean she didn't like to be taken care of.

"I've been busy," Corbeau said.

"Would it have killed you to wake me up when you left? A month ago?"

Corbeau felt a sudden wave of loneliness and guilt. An unkind person might say she was leading Sophie on by continuing to go home with her from time to time—except it had been going on so long, Sophie couldn't possibly have expectations beyond the occasional bout of mutual physical relief. Could she? After all, she had accused Corbeau more than once of using their back-and-forth as a way of avoiding anything of deeper significance. It was probably true, but Corbeau didn't have room in her life for anything significant. And the sex was enjoyable for both of them.

Corbeau touched the fur collar of Sophie's coat. Had it really been a month already? It seemed that just last week she was ducking out of Sophie's well-appointed apartment on Rue St. Dominique. She supposed it was about time they found each other again.

"You knew I wouldn't stay," she said.

Sophie regarded her for a moment then slipped her arm free. She cleared her throat. "This is the third incident in this area in a week." She flourished a pencil and a small notebook. "Has the great Elise Corbeau any theories?"

"None that I'm ready to share with the press."

"How about with an old friend?"

Corbeau let her gaze travel over the other woman's neat features, her perfectly arranged hair and spotless clothing. She could have gone home with her right then—back to Rue St. Dominique, to Persian carpets, Turkish sweets, and heady perfumes. Some pampering and a long nap would do her good about then. She just had to say the word—it was written all over Sophie's face.

But they'd been playing that game for years. If it hadn't stuck by now, it wasn't going to. It wasn't fair to either of them to keep their connection limping along like this. And all things considered, Corbeau really could do without the reminder of her past.

"I know better." Corbeau spun around and began to walk again. Sophie fell into step with her—no easy feat, considering how much longer Corbeau's legs were and how much more adequate to the task her footwear was. "Whatever I say to you will end up in whatever rag you sell it to, and Vautrin will have my head. He'd have had it a long time ago if the prefect's office hadn't stopped him."

"Why does the prefect's office care about you?"

Sophie stumbled on a loose cobblestone. Corbeau grasped her elbow before she tumbled into the muck. Sophie took the opportunity to insinuate herself beneath Corbeau's arm, pencil and paper at the ready.

"Don't know," Corbeau said. Sophie's small, tightly corseted waist felt right beneath her hand. "But I don't trust it. Javert is a man of the cloth and His Majesty's appointee. Once I've done the favor he's bound to ask of me, I'm sure I'll be out on my ear."

"I heard he's trying to rebuild the Bureau of Supernatural Investigations. Care to comment?"

"If he is, it'd be news to me."

Sophie opened her mouth to speak, but before she could say a word, a freshly painted fiacre pulled to a stop in front of them, spattering their skirts with a rancid stew of sewage and rainwater. Sophie flinched back with a little shriek, and the door opened.

"Inspector Corbeau," a man said from the darkness of the carriage. "Thought I'd find you here."

"Speak of the devil," Corbeau muttered.

Claude Javert, the prefect of police, leaned forward into the doorway. He was a sharp-featured man in his fifties with precisely trimmed salt-and-pepper hair and a thin mustache. He perched on the edge of his seat, long limbs folded like an excitable insect's. His smile and the lively intelligence in his eyes made him seem benign, but the impression was deceptive. Javert's ability to verbally eviscerate his enemies was matched only by his enjoyment of doing so.

Corbeau saw him register the newsmonger and the arm still around her waist. But he didn't comment.

"We haven't much time, Inspector. Get in."

Corbeau stood before the open door of the fiacre, blinking in the bright light of the carriage lamps, while Sophie melted back into the shadows. High-level functionaries of the King were no friends of the Left. Best for everyone if she slipped away before the prefect could put a name to her face.

How had Javert known Corbeau was there? What did he want?

It didn't matter. She had no choice now but to go with him.

Steeling herself, she stepped onto the carriage's metal footstep and slid onto the smooth leather bench. The door of the fiacre clicked shut beside her. A clap of thunder shook through the wood, and rain suddenly rushed down onto the street below. Prefect Javert rapped the carriage roof with the handle of his umbrella. Above them, the driver whistled and slapped the reins across the horse's back, and the carriage began to roll.

❖

"Your timing is impeccable, Monsieur," Corbeau said as she watched Sophie scurry for cover. She turned back to him. "How did you know I'd be here?"

"I looked first at Oubliette, but they told me you wouldn't be back until you'd settled a little matter of a broken chair and a bottle of red Bordeaux. Hmm. An agent in your position should know better than to be caught in establishments like that. And brawling like a common…" He shook his head. "Not at all the image the Sûreté wishes to project."

"What I do on my own time is my own affair, Monsieur."

"To the contrary, Inspector. The King considers public morality to be a top priority. And as a representative of His Majesty, your public comportment is most definitely his affair."

It was true, and there wasn't anything Corbeau could say about it. Every week, it seemed, Vautrin passed down another list of places, people, and activities forbidden to agents of the Sûreté. It was almost as much fun for him as his surprise inspections of the proof agents were required to produce on demand that they had recently confessed their sins to a priest. She was surprised the man hadn't resorted to bed checks.

Javert frowned, peering closer. "That's a nasty bruise. You ought to get some raw meat on that."

"Sure. The minute my salary allows me to afford meat."

"I'll look into it. We can't very well have you running to Jacques every month."

Corbeau was grateful that the darkness inside the carriage hid her embarrassment—embarrassment that made her want to shrink into the fine leather upholstery when the prefect tossed a small fabric pouch in her direction. The pouch landed on the seat beside her with the unmistakable clatter of coins. Ignoring it, Corbeau said, "You still didn't answer my question."

"You're not in a position to ask questions, Inspector. But if you insist, I knew that if you were half the officer your records suggest, you'd be on top of these disturbances. And I wasn't disappointed."

"I'd ask how you found out about tonight's disturbance, but if Chief Inspector Vautrin knew about it, all of Paris probably did."

Javert cocked an eyebrow. "Vautrin was there?"

"He and his priest hauled the victim off in a carriage, ranting about the devil's mark."

The prefect narrowed his eyes. "But you were investigating an uncontrolled flare of spiritual energy, correct?"

Corbeau frowned. Like Vautrin, Javert had been chosen in part because of his well-known religious convictions. She wouldn't have expected him to admit the possibility of spiritual energies, no less use terms Vidocq had coined.

"Vautrin shares the Church's opinion that any spiritual action not originating with the Church is from the Evil One," Corbeau said. "He also shares His Majesty's opinion that the police should be an arm of the Church." Corbeau would have thought Javert shared that opinion, but instead, here he was, throwing around Bureau terminology as if he had coined it.

Javert shook his head, frowning. "Were Monsieur Vidocq still with us, this never would have happened."

She wanted to say more—for instance, to point out that Javert himself was responsible for Vidocq's resignation. Had he named anyone else *commissaire de police*—anyone other than the one man whose mutual antipathy with Vidocq was legendary— Vidocq would still be chief inspector, the Bureau of Supernatural Investigations would still be in existence, and Gustave Vautrin would still be mucking out stables in some distant gendarmerie garrison.

But the prefect's office was the only thing standing between her and unemployment. She'd already said too much.

"You blame me for the new CP," he said, as if reading her thoughts. "Speak frankly, Inspector. At this point, my need for your services is far greater than any pleasure I might derive from punishing insult, I assure you."

Corbeau drew a deep breath, anger slamming against the desire for self-preservation. Diplomacy had never been her strong point, but she'd learned quickly, working in the Byzantine hierarchy of the Department of the Interior, to hold her tongue.

"By God, Inspector, what happened to your neck?"

Corbeau flinched as he reached out to touch the tender spots where Vautrin had tried to crush her windpipe with his baton. Shock and pain drove discretion from her mind.

"If you admired Chief Inspector Vidocq as much as your words suggest, you would have appointed your dog commissioner of police before Monsieur Duplessis," she spat. "And you'd have appointed your dog's fleas chief inspector before Gustave Vautrin. Duplessis is merely incompetent, but Vautrin is willfully pulling down everything Vidocq built, in the name of religion and his own vanity."

For a moment, the only sounds were the *clip-clop* of the horse's hooves on the pavement and the drumming of the rain on the roof of the carriage.

Then the prefect laughed.

"You don't know how refreshing it is to hear honesty from one's subordinates. Though I must point out that I was only responsible for Duplessis—not my first choice, by the way, but my hands were tied. Vautrin is the CP's fault. If it means anything, I tried any number of inducements to get Monsieur Vidocq to stay. The loss of the Bureau of Supernatural Investigations will be felt most grievously in weeks to come, I'm afraid."

"What do you mean?"

"You know exactly what I mean. These incidents—a cluster of outbursts among a diverse population in a small area—you can't tell me it's at all usual."

"So you know about the other ones?"

Javert nodded.

"And you think they're related?"

"Don't you?" he asked.

And yet he hadn't chosen to share that information with Vautrin, who had thought Armand Lambert possessed by the devil. Was it because Vautrin would have ignored the information? Or did Javert have a different agenda? Corbeau crossed her arms over her chest and settled herself more firmly against the high, padded back of the bench. Just how much did Javert know about the supernatural phenomena the Bureau had investigated? Aside from the Bureau's own records, safely under lock and key in Vidocq's possession—and a few texts rumored to be floating around Rome somewhere—Corbeau knew of no other documentation of the things they were discussing.

"These events are so unusual, in fact, that you've been investigating them against Vautrin's direct orders. Or what would have been his orders, if he'd had any inkling of what was going on. Of course something tells me if it wasn't this, you'd find something else to do against Vautrin's orders." Humor twinkled in his eyes.

"I'm doing my duty," Corbeau said.

"The chief inspector would probably beg to differ."

Corbeau fingered the bronze pin on the lapel of her coat. The pin was stamped with the Bureau insignia of bell, book, and candle. It was just a symbol now—a reminder of how far she had come—of what a girl from the slums could accomplish with brains and persistence. The pin was meaningless now but still a part of her. "I swore to protect the people of Paris from all threats natural and supernatural. Bringing the chief inspector his coffee does not further that goal."

A smile twitched at the edges of the prefect's lips. He drew a gold case from the interior breast pocket of his heavy coat. Inside was a row of Spanish cigarettes—an unexpected luxury in the hand of a public servant. She took one between her fingers and held it between her lips while he struck a lucifer. The violent shower of sparks made her jump. Why did he think it necessary to intimidate her with such a display when he surely carried a tinderbox like everyone else? But she bit back her remark, brushed the particles from her skirt as if she encountered sulfur matches every day, and let the rich aroma of Turkish tobacco fill her lungs.

As Javert lit one for himself, Corbeau imagined his bony fingers holding a quill to illuminate some ancient manuscript. Vautrin had washed out of seminary, Corbeau knew. But Javert, she had heard, had spent a couple of decades as a Jesuit before finding his calling intellectually stifling. Now he spent his days overseeing the broader affairs of the prefecture of police. Which again raised the question: why he would involve himself with the street-level goings on of a defunct sub-agency of a sub-agency?

"Inspector?"

"You're the only one who still calls me that. When Vautrin took the helm of the Sûreté, he made no secret that there was no longer a place for criminals or women."

"Vautrin's terminology is of no interest to me. I call things as they are. Or," he said, drawing deeply on his cigarette, "as they might well be called again."

Corbeau's heart raced. Was there actually a chance that she might regain her position at the Sûreté? Not wanting to seem too eager, she crossed her legs and leaned back against the smooth leather. She exhaled a hot plume toward the ceiling of the carriage and regarded him through a smoky veil.

"The Church speculates about angels dancing on pinheads," Javert said. "But the Bureau had actual, day-to-day experience of the supernatural. I knew Vautrin would shut it down, reassign the officers or let them go. But when it came to you, Inspector, I put my foot down. I made it clear you were not to be touched."

"Why?" she asked.

"All of the Bureau's agents saw action, but you were the only one who had experienced the supernatural on both sides of the law. You had a broader vision. You knew what it all meant, not from theory, training, or someone else's dogma, but from personal experience."

Corbeau blanched at the reminder of her criminal past. She'd worked hard to live it down, and having Javert mention it so casually—especially in light of her discoveries that morning—was like having a bandage removed before the scab was complete.

"This is why Chief Inspector Vautrin resents you so. He spent his whole time at seminary waiting to have a supernatural experience and never did. And then he meets you, convicted criminal and daughter of a witch, who can't escape the supernatural no matter how hard she tries."

Fury bubbled beneath Corbeau's embarrassment. *Witch* had been the term the neighbors had used when the culmination of their own misery had pushed them to find a scapegoat. By the time the mob came to drag her mother from their miserable little set of rooms, they had completely forgotten the infants she had safely delivered, the poultices and the healing tinctures she'd provided for much less than their worth.

Clearly unaware of her discomfort, Javert said, "I had to call in quite a few favors to keep you on. I hope you won't let me down."

Tendrils of smoke drifted up from the corners of his mouth as he regarded her through clear gray eyes. Corbeau had the impression she was a chess piece, and Javert was figuring out the most advantageous place to put her. It wasn't the best position to be in. On the other hand, if the prefect was hinting about reinstating her, she should at least be willing to hear him out.

"What do you need from me, Monsieur?"

"I want you to put the Montagne Ste. Geneviève out of your mind for the moment and have a look at this." Javert bent down to pull a paper envelope from the satchel near his feet. He handed it to her. "You've no doubt heard of Hermine Boucher," he said as she flipped through the collection of notes, sketches, and newspaper clippings inside.

"The prophetess of the Church of the Divine Spark?"

She withdrew an article written a year earlier, about a makeshift clinic the group had built near the ruins of the Bastille. The organization had acquired a physician, the article stated—a physician skilled in addressing spiritual as well as physical complaints. They took no money for their work, which had endeared them to the public, though their attempts at spiritual healing had drawn condemnation from the local bishop and the King. In the accompanying sketch, Corbeau recognized Madame Boucher, whose athletic, almost mannish build and taste for the light, loosely corseted gowns her mother might have favored had been a gift to cartoonists and satirists alike.

"She disappeared several days ago," Javert said.

Corbeau looked up from the papers. "Was His Majesty behind it?"

"Not that I know of," Javert said in a way that suggested if it were the case, he *would* have known. "Madame Boucher's group is well loved by the masses. She herself is well loved—

glamorous, young, pretty, and tragically widowed. His Majesty is too smart to make a martyr out of her. But he's not anxious for her return. If it were up to him, I think he'd be happy for her to remain gone, and the group to simply fade away."

"Maybe that would be best."

Javert frowned at her.

"I'm surprised at you, Inspector. I'd have thought, above all, you'd want to see justice done. Fortunately, the decision to investigate does not reside with you, or with His Majesty. It resides with me. And I need your help finding her, quietly and before the papers get wind of this."

"Why the secrecy? People disappear all the time. Why not put Vautrin on it?"

"Vautrin's assistant took the initial report. He concluded that—" Javert cleared his throat and leaned in conspiratorially, "Madame Boucher was kidnapped with the aid of black magic."

"You believe that?"

"From the report, it certainly seems possible."

Corbeau scoffed. "Vautrin thinks anything he can't explain is black magic."

"But in this case, he may be right. And if black magic is actually afoot, I'm glad he kicked it up to me, because he has no business investigating it himself."

Corbeau sat back and took a long pull from her cigarette. "It would serve him right for getting rid of Vidocq."

"But it would serve the rest of us very badly. Most people remember a time when there was no organized civil police force."

"Then they remember how you couldn't walk down most streets in broad daylight."

"They also remember a tax being raised to pay for a police force. The panic that would ensue if word of Madame Boucher's, shall we say *irregular disappearance*, became common knowledge would make people forget we cut the crime rate in half. People are out of work and prices are rising fast, sometimes doubling in the space of a day. People are already pissing their pants in the Montagne Ste. Geneviève. If it gets out that the angel of the

Church of the Divine Spark was spirited away by demonic forces, and the police could do nothing about it, the hysteria will spread across the entire city. That kind of panic left you an orphan. There will be many more orphans, throughout Paris. And the people will blame us, Inspector."

And as much as Corbeau hated to admit it, she knew he was right. It wasn't the time to stand back and watch Vautrin hang himself with his own stupidity and shortsightedness, much as she would have relished it. There was just one problem. "You seem to forget, Monsieur, that I've been demoted to Vautrin's girl-of-all-work."

"Leave Vautrin to me. I have a good idea who has taken Madame Boucher and why. Make the case, bring her in, and you'll never have to worry about Vautrin again."

"Her?"

Javert motioned for her to pass the papers. He riffled through the articles and notes until his fingers came to a well-worn newspaper sketch. Two elegantly dressed women stood before one of the most expensive shops on the Boulevard St. Germain. The one on the left—a strong-featured blonde in her late twenties— Corbeau recognized as Hermine Boucher. The other woman was smaller and more simply dressed. Her face was turned to one side, and a fur hat partially hid straight, dark hair, which ended, bluntly and shockingly, at the level of her chin.

The young widow of Henri Boucher was renowned for her beauty, but it was the other woman who caught Corbeau's eye. The artist had captured a certain haughtiness in her stature—as if her plain dress and short hair were a daring style choice, rather than, as was more likely the case, indications that financial desperation had once forced her to sell her hair and finer clothing. The way she was drawn also betrayed a sly intelligence. Corbeau wasn't surprised to see the title "Doctor" beside the woman's name.

"Dr. Maria Kalderash. The artist drew her looking to the side in order to hide her deformity," Javert said.

"The doctor working in the slums with the Divine Spark?"

Javert nodded. "In reality, Dr. Kalderash's face is noticeably scarred. She also wears a mechanical device on the right side."

"The Eye," Corbeau said. Somewhere in the back of her mind, she remembered hearing about the doctor and her eccentric prosthetic gadgets. Although the articles in Javert's hand spoke of the ones she'd created for healing purposes, there had also been a series of devices that amounted to fashion accessories. For a short time, they had been quite a sensation among the moneyed classes. It was rumored that the contraption she herself wore enabled her to see through a blinded eye.

"Dr. Kalderash trained as a physician in her native Romania. During the year or so that she was associated with the Church of the Divine Spark, she worked side by side with Madame Boucher. Her association with the Church ended some time ago, but she still maintains a modest clientele. Her training isn't recognized here, of course. Her methods are…foreign at best. Spiritually, they are suspect."

"You're calling her a witch?" Corbeau asked. Javert raised a conciliatory hand at her tone.

"Under His Majesty's new guidelines regarding the prosecution of witchcraft, the argument could be made. However, I have no intention of leveling those charges against her—not when I believe her to be culpable in the more concrete case of Madame Boucher's disappearance."

Corbeau looked at the newspaper sketch again. It was dated the previous January. More of the story came back to her. Two of Kalderash's devices—the Gin Liver and the Discreet Lady's Stomach Bypass—had been at the height of their popularity. Her name and Boucher's had always seemed to be linked then. But that had changed over the summer. Corbeau had marked the devices' decline in popularity as the passing of another trend.

Had it been something more than that?

"They were lovers, you know," Javert said, interrupting her thoughts.

He said the word matter-of-factly, and without the revulsion or judgment she would have expected from a former priest. Corbeau glanced at the sketch again, her eyes lingering on Dr. Kalderash. Something about the picture stirred her. She'd always had a weakness for intelligent women. She'd even pursued a few. But that had been when she was younger, had more money and energy, and before it had just become easier to be alone.

Javert teased another clipping from the pile of papers and slid it on top of the first. In this sketch, Madame Boucher stood at the entrance of a large, well-appointed home. Beneath a fortune of exquisite pelts, she wore a simple gown—a light, flowing fabric decorated with thousands of crystal beads. It was of the same old-fashioned design—lightly corseted, without the full skirts and bustles her fashionable peers favored. As if to compensate, her light hair had been swept up in a complicated knot and adorned with jewels.

"Three nights ago, Madame Boucher attended a party. Dr. Kalderash turned up uninvited. There was some unpleasantness between them, and Dr. Kalderash was unceremoniously ejected. Much later, Madame stepped into her carriage and vanished."

"Vanished?"

Javert pinched out what remained of his cigarette and ground the remaining paper twist underfoot.

"The footman reported he shut the door behind Madame, and when he opened it again upon arriving home, the carriage was empty. He said he didn't stop at any point along the journey. So you can see why people are rumbling about black magic. It doesn't help that Dr. Kalderash is of Gypsy extraction."

"But do you actually believe she used black magic to kidnap a woman from a moving vehicle?" Corbeau asked, incredulous.

"That's what I intend to find out. I thought you might interview her this morning." He smiled at her expression. "The universe is a big place, Inspector, with more possibilities than our mustard-seed-sized intellects can conceive."

"But you consider Kalderash a strong suspect?"

"I consider her the only suspect."

"I thought the universe was a big place. Surely it's large enough for more than one theory at this point in the investigation."

Javert shrugged. "I'll make it worth your while. Review the facts of the case. Interview the suspect and whomever else you deem important. I'll keep Vautrin out of your hair while you do. And when you gather enough evidence for an arrest warrant for Dr. Kalderash, then you'll have the opportunity to carry out that warrant as a fully restored detective inspector of the Sûreté."

Corbeau let out a long breath. Her windpipe still ached from where Vautrin had tried to crush it. A lump was forming on the back of her skull from where he'd bashed it against the doorjamb. Hadn't he been surprised, when he'd arrived at Armand Lambert's building, priest in tow, to see that she'd gotten there first? Whatever dark little business of his she'd stumbled on, he'd be looking for any excuse to send her on her way. She certainly didn't fancy spending the day skulking around the Palais de Justice trying to avoid him.

At the same time, Javert's certainty of Dr. Kalderash's guilt suggested a setup. It wasn't as if she hadn't set up suspects before, of course. The first thing an agent learned was that if a criminal isn't guilty of the crime in question, he—or she—is probably guilty of something else. But it smelled all the same.

"I've done a lot of your research for you already," Javert said. "I'm confident that once you read the evidence, you'll agree with me. What do you think, Inspector?"

He held out his hand. She hesitated. Surely he didn't expect her to accept his assessment on faith. Yet she might arrive at the same place Javert had, through her own methods. And then her days of coffee and paperwork would be over.

"I'll read over your reports," she said, taking the proffered hand. "But I'll conduct my own investigation."

"I wouldn't expect anything less."

"What about Mr. Lambert?"

"Who?"

"Armand Lambert. You showed up at his house just as I was leaving. Chief Inspector Vautrin and his pet priest took Mr. Lambert into custody earlier this morning following his outburst. Who knows what sort of spiritual remediation they have in mind for him? Frankly, Monsieur, I fear for his safety."

"Mmm." Javert nodded. "You concentrate on Dr. Kalderash. I'll find your Mr. Lambert. In the meantime, I believe you know where you are now." He rapped the top of the carriage with the handle of a large, oiled-silk umbrella. The carriage slowed and pulled to a stop before the café Corbeau knew so well. "Oubliette doesn't open for another hour or two. It should give you plenty of time to settle your affairs there before you go to interview Dr. Kalderash. Best not to let these things fester. Her address is inside, by the way. The Rue des Rosiers. Although I'm sure you could have deduced that for yourself."

Corbeau folded the papers back into their envelope and tucked it into her shoulder bag. Javert opened the door onto the uneven sidewalk in front of the café. Corbeau placed one foot onto the metal step, pausing to watch the pounding rain and the river rushing through the gutter beneath her. Javert chuckled, his voice resonant within the wooden walls of the fiacre.

"Where are my manners?" He handed her his umbrella. When she hesitated, he said, "Use it in good health, Inspector. Return it to me at our next meeting. And don't forget this." He handed her the purse of coins she had earlier ignored. "I won't lose my only qualified agent over a matter of two weeks' pay."

Reluctantly, Corbeau tucked the purse into her coat pocket. As the carriage rolled off, she wrestled the baleen frame of the umbrella into position, taking comfort in the silk shelter, though by that time, her hems were soaked through. Dodging puddles and the occasional pedestrian, she swallowed her pride and made her way to the front door.

## CHAPTER FOUR

Though Corbeau would have allowed at least a week to pass before turning up at Oubliette again—she would have needed at least that much time to scrounge the money she owed for the chair and the bottle of Bordeaux—Javert was right. It was better to sort these things out before they got out of control. The owner, Marie, would forgive her once she had cash in hand. And from the weight of the coins in her pocket, she likely had enough to settle up with Ugly Jacques as well. After she cleared her accounts, she'd go home and sleep all day. Perhaps all night, too. Her employment was no longer at the whim of Chief Inspector Vautrin. No matter that he probably wished her dead now—Javert wouldn't let him touch her.

The café's dark-blue awning whipped back and forth in the wind. Cold drops dripped from the sodden canvas, falling hard on the oiled silk of Javert's umbrella as she passed beneath it. The café had closed for the night around two. Corbeau reckoned it was a little after seven. The important thing was that Marie would be happy to take her money any time of day. Despite the sign, the front door was unlocked. Corbeau walked past the stacked chairs and tables that would fill the narrow stretch of sidewalk out front should it ever stop raining. As she shut the door behind her, the sounds of food preparation stopped, the kitchen door burst open, and a stout, formidable-looking woman charged out.

"Well, don't you have a nerve?" Marie looked as if she'd slept as little as Corbeau had, but it showed more clearly on her rough-featured face and in the sag of her age-rounded shoulders. "I thought I told you—"

"Peace, Madame. I came to pay you, and to apologize."

The juggernaut of a woman stopped short, sharp eyes lighting on the pouch Corbeau held up. A smile spread across her face at the jingle of the coins inside. The smile grew wider with every coin Corbeau pressed into her fleshy palm.

"And one more for your trouble," Corbeau said. "I am truly sorry, Madame. It won't happen again."

Marie held her gaze for a moment, then nodded, satisfied. "Thank you, dear, I knew you'd come through."

"I'm sure that's what you told everyone last night after you threw me out."

"Well…now…" She self-consciously tucked a strand of steel-colored hair back beneath her frayed scarf. "What's a woman to do? You were much better at paying your bills when you were a bum, you know."

"Of course back then you always complained about the 'element' my business attracted."

"Would have broken your mother's heart. All that knowledge twisted and turned to immoral purpose." She cocked her head, thoughtful. "Though I can't say she'd have liked your current activities any better. Police work, indeed."

"You have to admit it does keep people on their best behavior knowing the Sûreté is about."

"Except when it's the Sûreté turning the place on its ear."

Corbeau closed her eyes and exhaled slowly. "I've just paid for that and more."

"Well…now…" Marie smiled and patted her arm. "I suppose you have made up for it. And you've done so much for that poor woman in the Montagne Ste. Geneviève. How is her little boy?"

Corbeau exhaled a breath of relief. Marie was one of the few people who still knew her from the old days. She'd been a friend of Corbeau's mother. Corbeau had practically grown up in the warmth of the wooden walls and the glow of the wall sconces. The café was a refuge whose loss Corbeau would have felt acutely. "A nuisance. But he's doing well."

"I'm glad. It was bad enough, him running under the wheels of that wagon. I never thought a little one like that would survive an amputation on top of it."

Corbeau was grateful Marie hadn't reminded her Joseph had been running because Corbeau had been chasing him. The fumes from her tinctures and potions had been slowly curdling her common sense, pushing her natural suspicion toward a deadly paranoia. When six-year-old Joseph's curiosity had led him to peek through the window of Corbeau's basement lab that day, he'd been lucky the carriage had gotten him before Corbeau had. Vidocq had kicked down the door of her lab the next day.

"Joseph's a tough little weasel," Corbeau said.

Marie narrowed her eyes at the uncharacteristic emotion in her voice. She caught her eye. "You're doing right by that family, Elise. Your mother would be proud."

Corbeau sighed. "I won't be doing it for long if prices keep doubling every time I take a breath. If His Majesty doesn't give our salaries a bump soon, I'll be sleeping on the floor of Joseph's bedroom—and I'll still be paying that place off, poltergeists and all."

Marie smiled kindly and patted her arm again.

"Come to the bar and I'll fix you some breakfast. On the house. You look terrible, by the way."

Corbeau followed her across the traffic-worn floorboards to the bar at the back. Leaning Javert's umbrella against the bar, she slid onto one of the stools. She grimaced at her reflection in the long mirror on the wall. Bruises shaped like Vautrin's fingers were blooming on her neck. They matched the black eye Jacques's man had given her. Not the most attractive look, but at least she hadn't lost any teeth. She ran her fingers through her hair until it no longer looked like a bird's nest and took a clean cloth napkin from the pile on the edge of the bar to wipe the dirt from her face. A little banged up, but not bad for twenty-eight, she thought. A proper wash, and she'd be good as new. She turned up the collar of her coat and winked at her reflection.

"Jacques hasn't sent anyone else, has he?" Corbeau called. She used the mirror to give the place a quick once-over.

"Pfft. After what you did to the last one? Besides, I don't think drooling thugs wake up as early as honest citizens such as ourselves."

After a bit of shuffling behind the kitchen doors, Marie reappeared with a slice of buttered bread on a plate, a wedge of cheese, and a small cup of strong coffee. The bread was stale, but it calmed the burn in Corbeau's stomach. The mere smell of the coffee began to clear her head.

"That's better, yes?" Marie asked.

Corbeau smiled gratefully around a mouthful of cheese. She flipped another coin onto the lacquered wood in response and took out the papers Javert had given her, spreading them across the bar in front of her. Nodding her understanding, Marie pocketed the coin and drifted back into the kitchen.

As she took the clippings from the envelope, Corbeau admired the clean, thick paper. The envelope had seen a lot of use but had a lot of use left in it still. Javert's notes were likewise written on expensive stock. He had taken great care quartering and tearing the sheets of paper inside—paper covered on both sides with perfectly straight lines of his small, neat hand.

The prefect's salary was doubtless larger than her own, but she was willing to wager not by enough to afford Spanish cigarettes and expensive paper. Many of Corbeau's colleagues had taken second jobs. But Javert was high enough on the ladder that such an infraction would be noticed—noticed and not tolerated. Yet he didn't strike her as a man who lived beyond his means. The discrepancy vexed her, but she would have to tuck the question away for later.

Right now, she had a case before her for the first time since Vidocq had resigned.

Javert had organized the papers starting with the clipping showing Madame Boucher at the party where she'd last been seen. She rubbed the newspaper between her fingers. Unlike Javert's paper, it was cheap and thin, and left a grayish residue on her skin. A few pages later she found the police report. Interesting. The report contained a summary of the events as told to one of Vautrin's new hires by members of Hermine Boucher's staff. First, Corbeau would have expected Vautrin himself to take the report for what would surely become a high-profile case. Second, she would have expected to find extended interviews with the driver and footman, who would have been the last people to see Madame Boucher, rather than a few sentences summarizing what other employees had said. The driver wasn't even mentioned. Corbeau went through the notes again and again, but found no further interviews or investigation of the employees. Corbeau shook her head. Sloppy work from an inexperienced officer. It was going to cost the investigation.

Disgusted, she laid the report aside and started another pile for newspaper clippings. Several concerned Dr. Kalderash, ranging from her work with the Church of the Divine Spark to dark speculations about her origins and secret spiritual practices. One such piece referred to Kalderash, rather insultingly, as a "Gypsy necromancer." *Dangerous talk to titillate the masses*, Corbeau thought. It was more likely than Kalderash trafficking with the dead that whoever had sold that particular tidbit to the paper had thought to gain a few extra sou in shock value. Still, she would have to be careful when interviewing the suspect about her practices. The Church might not see a difference between summoning spirits and pretending to see the future in tea leaves, but when it came to arresting a woman for a serious crime, that could make all the difference in the world.

She found a few interesting articles about a free clinic opening near the Montagne Ste. Geneviève. The Church of the Divine Spark had funded its construction, and Dr. Maria Kalderash would serve as the primary physician. Most of the articles hailed Madame

Boucher as some sort of saint. A few expressed doubt about Dr. Kalderash's qualifications, as well as about the "spiritual" care that the clinic would provide along with basic medical services.

Kalderash's departure from the Divine Spark seemed to be of much greater interest to the gossip-slingers than her charitable works. One long article, a masterpiece of prurient speculation, blamed Kalderash for everything from the closure of the clinic to the latest cholera outbreak. The article consisted of the same piecemeal assembly of information purchased bit by bit from different unnamed, unverifiable sources—people like Sophie, who lurked in cafés, parks, and places of amusement with open ears and ready pencils. Despite the unabashed glee with which the author had documented the destruction of Dr. Kalderash's professional reputation following her falling-out with Madame Boucher, the collected snatches of gossip contained some solid information.

Nobody was quite certain when Maria Kalderash had come to Paris—though surely the information could be found somewhere in the bowels of the Palais de Justice. She had burst onto the social scene a year and a half earlier with the introduction of the Gin Liver, a small, removable device the size of a potato, which filtered alcohol out of the body as quickly as a person could drink it down. It had become wildly popular with a certain class of rakish young men and had made Dr. Kalderash, by all accounts, fabulously wealthy herself. A companion device, the Discreet Lady's Stomach Bypass, allowed young women of breeding to eat to satisfaction while siphoning off any sort of unseemly excess before it attached itself to their nubile forms. The article made no mention of how the devices connected to the body. Corbeau made a note to find out.

As she followed the clippings back through time, a story began to emerge. At some point, a little less than two years earlier, the widow Hermine Boucher had discovered an obscure inventor whose immense talent apparently made up for her foreign birth, dubious dearth of connections, and appalling lack of money.

Despite these differences—and the scandal of Dr. Kalderash's heathen blood—the women became inseparable. Boucher funded Kalderash's growing business—creating cosmetic enhancements for the vain and deep-pocketed—and used her share of the profits to start her church.

Though the names of Boucher and Kalderash had peppered the pages of the scandal sheets for quite a while, discussions of the beliefs and practices of the Divine Spark were conspicuously absent, though Javert's notes addressed themselves to this organization. By Javert's account, Madame Boucher's interest in the occult had begun following the death of her husband. That wasn't uncommon. Corbeau remembered numerous occasions when neighbors and acquaintances had sought out her mother's assistance to contact a recently departed loved one. But rather than fading over time, Madame Boucher's interest deepened. She began to gather others around her, to style herself as some sort of medium. Shortly after Dr. Kalderash joined her entourage, Javert's unnamed sources reported that the group had taken a political bent, setting itself, philosophically at least, against the Church and the reactionary King. It was here that Javert's speculations left off.

And then, at some point last winter, Kalderash's name, which had been linked inextricably with that of Madame Boucher in the papers, had suddenly disappeared from mention. It was as if the inventor had been called into existence on Boucher's whim, then dismissed when the whim had changed.

Hermine Boucher had kept some very prominent company, Corbeau thought. As dizzying as such a meteoric rise into society must have been for someone like Kalderash, who had likely grown up around caravans and campfires, it must have been humiliating to be dropped so unceremoniously. The effect upon her business must have been even harder to bear. Lives were ruined when people like Hermine Boucher called an end to a fashion.

"Hmm," Corbeau said. Maybe Javert was being honest with her. If the women had been lovers, their falling-out would have been devastating on a very personal level as well. Stabbed in the back in business, friendship, and love. Many people would kill over just one of those.

"Sounds like someone's working hard," a voice said behind her.

Corbeau turned, quickly gathering up the papers in front of her. "You following me, Soph?"

But Corbeau felt a smile pulling at the corners of her mouth. The woman's presence was inevitable, for one thing. For another, Sophie was another of the few remaining faces from the old days. If they'd met as adults, Corbeau wouldn't have allowed a gossipmonger within ten feet of her. But Sophie had kept her confidences well—better than Corbeau would have expected. With breakfast inside her, and a long nap in sight, everything was looking a lot less bleak. Leaning on an elbow, Corbeau looked at her first lover, and the smile crept all the way across her face.

Sophie smiled back. Morning's light made it easier to appreciate the care she had taken with her appearance. Her cream-colored silk gown was untouched by the rain. Over it, she wore a long, form-hugging crimson redingote decorated with rows of silver buttons that gave the over-garment a smart, military look. She had removed her very expensive coat and hung it near the door with her umbrella.

"God, you're a sight for sore eyes."

"And you just look sore." Sophie gestured toward her bruised face. "Have your misdeeds finally caught up with you?"

Corbeau nodded. She wasn't ready to discuss her scuffle with Vautrin or what it might have meant. Her past might have been off limits, but Sophie considered police business fair game. Better she should blame the bruises and scratches on Ugly Jacques—at least until Corbeau figured out why Vautrin was so keen on personally presiding over exorcisms on the wrong side of town.

Corbeau flinched when Sophie's cool fingers traced the goose egg on her cheek, but she bit back the sharp remark that had been her first instinct. She'd spent her adolescence fending for herself in the fetid little streets around the Bastille; it had taken a long time to learn to let someone take care of her. The people she'd allowed had been few and far between. But after the night she'd had, even she had to admit that a little babying would do her good.

As if reading her mind, Sophie laid a hand on her cheek and said, "Why don't you come back to my rooms and rest for a bit? I'm sure Vautrin can get his own coffee for one day."

"What, no drinks first? No banter? What kind of girl do you think I am?"

Sophie's smile softened. "The kind who could use a hot bath and a few hours' sleep between silk sheets."

Corbeau laughed in spite of herself. "You do know, then."

The well-tended fingers traveled down her neck, down her arm, and rested on her wrist. Sophie had rubbed tinted oil into her fingernails. They glowed a warm, translucent red. "Only that, if you like. No expectations, Elise."

Their fingers found each other and tangled. They had agreed years ago: no promises, no expectations. The times they'd tried to make it more than that had been disastrous. But neither fact ever made it easier to leave in the morning. All the same, the pull of Sophie's sweetly scented flesh was almost irresistible—flesh that she knew almost as well as her own. She had known so little safety in her life. The safety of the familiar, even if it wasn't perfect, called to her.

"I'll think about it," Corbeau said, sliding her hand free.

Sophie pulled up the stool beside her and crossed what Corbeau knew to be very shapely legs beneath her dress. The ensemble probably cost some admirer more than what Corbeau made in a month.

"Don't you have some bankers to harass or something?" Corbeau asked.

"Silly. You're much more interesting these days. Why don't you tell me what's going on in the Montagne Ste. Geneviève?"

"If you knew to show up there this morning, then you know as much as I do. More than that, I couldn't tell you."

"Because it's police business?" Sophie asked.

"Because I have no idea myself. But ghoulies and ghosties aren't your usual beat. What's your interest?"

"Let's just say my interest is personal."

Sophie arched her back like a cat in the sun. Suppressing a grin at the other woman's transparency, Corbeau forced herself to look away. "Well, if you learn anything new about the disturbances, I hope you'll let me know. In the meantime, I do have some questions that may be more up your alley."

Sophie looked distinctly pleased at the thought. She patted her hair and leaned in on an elbow. "Anything for you, Inspector."

"What do you know about Hermine Boucher?"

Surprise and pleasure lit Sophie's face. "Ooh, are you working on that? I wouldn't have thought Vautrin would let you near such a high-profile case with a ten-foot barge pole."

"Vautrin has nothing to do with it."

"Working on your own, then? You never could resist a damsel in distress."

"Just answer the question, Soph. Who wants her gone?"

Sophie picked up Corbeau's empty coffee cup and tipped it sideways to watch the sludge ooze across the bottom. "A lot of people. The King, for one. Oh, he's no fan of the Divine Spark, that's for sure. Besides, the Great Prophet—that's Hermine—scares people. It doesn't come across in the newspaper sketches, but she has this power about her. When she looks at you, it's as if she can see through you, into your past and into the future." She met Corbeau's eyes. "Power like that often frightens those in authority, especially if their authority is illegitimate."

"Hermine, is it?"

Sophie blushed. Her familiarity in referring to Madame Boucher by her given name wasn't lost on Corbeau. Nor was her uncharacteristic enthusiasm for the idea of spiritual power. Sophie had always reserved a special disdain for religion. Until now, Corbeau had assumed that disdain extended to the supernatural as well. Sophie shrugged. "The Great Prophet doesn't stand on ceremony, even with us lowly gossipmongers."

"Yes, she does quite a bit of work on the behalf of the lowly, doesn't she?"

"And the King doesn't like it, not one bit."

"No, nor her group's unorthodox beliefs, I suppose. But with the noise the rabble are making about rising prices and new moral restrictions coming down from the throne, I doubt His Majesty would risk making a martyr of her," Corbeau said.

"Yes, that's true." A wicked glint lit Sophie's eyes. "The Church calls her 'the Whore of Babylon,' you know."

"Babylon the Great, Mother of all Harlots and Abominations?"

"You've heard the sermons?"

"No, that's what Vautrin calls me. When he's in a good mood."

Sophie smiled. "Of course those are the exact words that Hermine uses to describe the Church. There's scriptural evidence to back that up, by the way. It's not just a convenient insult."

"So, some bishop on a mission, then."

Sophie cocked her head, frowning. "Maybe, but Hermine's group isn't really big enough to be a threat. Not yet, at least."

"What about their beliefs?"

Sophie reached for Corbeau's bread and took a thoughtful bite. "The Great Prophet believes that God uses spirits to speak to us. Of course the Evil One also uses spirits to possess and torment and confuse. It's not always easy to discern which is which. And then there are all the usual charlatans."

"So a person needs a wise leader like Hermine Boucher to show them the difference."

"Exactly. And don't talk with your mouth full. It's coarse."

Corbeau paused to swallow the remainder of the dry bread, wishing she had a drop of coffee left to wash it down. After her breakfast had scratched its way down to her stomach, she said, "How can you tell if someone is speaking for God, or if they're just after your money?"

"Oh, Hermine is for real," Sophie said. "I've seen it."

Corbeau leaned back, half-listening as Sophie went on to describe a dozen astounding supernatural feats she had seen the missing woman perform. A few Corbeau identified as advanced stage tricks. Others Corbeau had witnessed herself in the course of her work, although she wouldn't have described them in terms of spirits acting through people. From Corbeau's experience, many of the things people blamed on spirits were unconscious manifestations of an individual's vital spiritual forces. But it wasn't this difference in terminology that nagged at the back of her mind. What bothered her was the light in Sophie's eyes—the gleam of the true believer—as Sophie spoke of the missing Madame Boucher.

"You keep speaking of her in the present tense." Corbeau interrupted Sophie's monologue. "The woman has been missing for several days without a ransom demand. It's not looking good."

Sophie stopped short and smiled patronizingly. "If you'd seen what I have, you'd have a little faith, Inspector."

"I've seen that and more. If anything, it discourages faith. You sound very taken with this woman."

Sophie's smile turned brittle. "No business of yours. I admire her, that's all. She's very powerful, and she's used her power to help a lot of people. Actually, you'd find this interesting. It's sort of the other side of what you used to do. You used to help people channel spirits—"

"I did nothing of the sort—"

"You know you did. You just called it something else. Of course you didn't care as long as it was making you money."

"Money you didn't mind spending. But that's not the point. My formulae helped people to develop what was already inside—"

"They came to you for help, and how many ended up in the madhouse or in the grave?"

"They came to me for a quick path to power. I gave it to them."

Why did so many of their discussions turn into a fight?

"They came to you for help," Sophie insisted. "But Hermine actually does help people. She helps them keep the spirits away."

"Really?" Corbeau quickly forgot their argument. If Sophie was correct, Madame Boucher had been working the reverse of

Corbeau's own research. Where Corbeau's potions had brought out her clients' latent supernatural abilities, Hermine Boucher was helping people suppress them. "How?"

"Do you remember, Bernadette?" Sophie asked, suddenly, irritatingly switching the subject. "That little basement in Montmartre? When it was just the two of us?"

"I told you never to call me that."

"Relax, there's no one around but Marie, and she's not talking. I miss those days. You do, too. Sleeping all day, champagne all night—remember?"

"That was you. I spent my nights in the lab."

"Not all of them. Don't you miss it, Elise?"

Corbeau ground her teeth in frustration. She wanted to steer the conversation back to the Church of the Divine Spark, but she couldn't resist setting Sophie straight. "Which part? Holed up for fourteen hours at a time nursing a still in a poorly ventilated basement, or spending the rest of the time hiding from the people who wanted to kill me and take my recipes? Hard to remember which part was more fun."

"I meant the part where it was you and me against the world."

Corbeau sighed. Slowly the fighting urge began to drain away. She did remember that part, and not without fondness. But it was too late and too much water under the bridge. "We've tried that, Soph. It never quite works out, though, does it?"

"Only because you're a tyrant."

"And because you won't do as you're told."

They glared at each other for a moment. Sophie cracked a smile and looked away, shaking her head.

"What about Maria Kalderash?" Corbeau asked.

The smile faded. Sophie set her jaw in the defiant way that Corbeau knew well.

"If you're looking for a murderer, Inspector, look no further than that witch."

"Wait. Who said anything about a murder? What do you know?"

"All I'm saying is that if anyone would want to do Hermine harm, it would be that woman."

"Why?"

Corbeau could think of a handful of reasons, all neatly presented in Javert's dossier. But Javert had put the articles together. Javert had an agenda. Additional information would help Corbeau to better evaluate where fact left off and Javert's desire to arrest Dr. Kalderash began.

"Hermine brought that Gypsy chit up from the gutter and right into her house. She introduced those ridiculous contraptions into society and made Kalderash's name synonymous with fashion. Then when it came time to return the favor, the good doctor begged off on some high-and-mighty scruples."

"What did she want Kalderash to do?"

Sophie looked thoughtful. "I'm not sure. But whatever it was, she wouldn't do it, and Hermine was furious. That's why they parted ways."

"Sounds like Madame Boucher had more of a reason to turn murderer than the Gypsy," Corbeau said.

Sophie frowned. Clearly she hadn't realized that this was the logical conclusion of her statement. "I'm just telling you what happened, Inspector. That woman stabbed Hermine in the back. There was bad blood between them, and I wouldn't be surprised if whatever happened, the Gypsy was behind it."

"I see."

"Now I've told you everything I know," she said, smoothing down her redingote and trying to sound pleasant again. "Won't you come back to my rooms, Elise? Let me spoil you for an hour or two."

Corbeau regarded her for a long moment. Sophie had passed her some good information, though she'd had to argue it out of her. She was also disturbed by how close Sophie seemed to be to the situation. If this were only a bit of tittle-tattle she'd picked up here and there, she'd have no cause to get so worked up over it. And she was far too impressed with Madame Boucher to be entirely objective.

On the other hand, there was a chance that, given time and the proper inducements, Sophie might remember something more. Corbeau's head pounded. Sophie laid a hand on her forearm.

"And later, if you're really interested, I might be persuaded to tell you where the Divine Spark is meeting this very night."

Corbeau snapped to attention. A look of victory crossed Sophie's face, and she covered Corbeau's hand with her own.

"You wouldn't lie about something like that."

"Never."

Corbeau exhaled heavily. Most agents persuaded their informants with coin. Of course with Sophie, she was never sure who was bribing whom. She lifted Sophie's palm to her lips. "Just this once. I mean it. I'll be by in a couple of hours, but right now I have something to take care of."

## CHAPTER FIVE

Maria had awakened before the rain. The early hours of that cold November morning had greeted her with darkness, chill, and the tingling, metallic smell that always reminded her of blood. There had been too much blood, hers and other people's, spilled over stupid things recently. And violence had followed her all her life—which is why she had sat up in her narrow bed, beneath the sloping ceiling of her converted attic bedroom on the Rue des Rosiers, and resigned herself to the new day even before it had truly begun. Violence was coming. It was no time to be lazy.

Pulling a quilted velvet robe over her nightdress, she padded toward the stairs. The robe had been one of her first purchases in Paris. One of her only luxuries. Spending half her life up to her elbows in metal and grease, and the other half on the run, left little room for nice things. Still, the robe was comfortable and soundly made. It had served her well.

She navigated the stairwell one-eyed and in the dark. The loss of both depth perception and light made even a well-traveled staircase treacherous. She went slowly.

Her home was modest, and the common areas were tidy—although since Hermine had driven her business away, the areas that once welcomed visitors were gradually but inexorably giving way to her research. And research was messy. The hallway, though, remained sparse: a few icons on the walls—more to remind her of home than for the sake of any religious sentiment—and a lamp on a spindly table. But the front room, which she had once kept neat for her customers, was now a shambling, cluttered extension of her basement lab.

She took the hall lamp from its stand, lit it, and set it on the edge of the desk before the front window. Her Eye was on the table, where she'd left it before retiring. Despite the soft leather band, the apparatus was heavy, and by the end of the day, she was ready to sacrifice sight just to be rid of it. She carefully wiped clean the smooth skin the doctors had pulled over the naked socket. Chief Inspector Vautrin hadn't realized the Gypsy to whom he was teaching a lesson had official sanction to be in Paris. The physician he'd summoned had done a good job covering the damage, but Maria was still waiting for an apology.

She wiped the woven metal that sat between the device and her skin, then buckled the band around her head. The cool mesh met her face with its usual electrical sizzle. She was accustomed to the sensation by now, but it was never comfortable. The Eye clicked and whirred, and the room flickered into three dimensions of color, shadow, and light.

Like the table against the adjacent wall, Maria's desk was invisible beneath stacks of notes, journals, and books. She'd managed to restrict the tools to the basement, but only out of necessity. Customers no longer filed in and out of the front room, not since Hermine had slandered her name and her work to the empty-headed aristos, who had, at one time, vied to be first to strap on her latest toy. It was just as well. The recreational prosthetics had helped her keep a roof over her head and stash away a suitcase full of money for the next time she had to flee and start anew. But she'd found the work meaningless and trite. She was glad it was over.

The plans for the *Left Hand of Justice* lay across her desk where she'd left them when her head had started pounding and she'd grown weary of looking at them. The Eye fixed on the long sheet of paper, edges curling up beneath the books she'd used to weight the corners down. The lenses turned to adjust themselves to her small, neat handwriting. Justice. It was a joke. The thing was at the root of all of her troubles, and it hadn't even been built yet. A weapon like that should never be built. It had been idiotic to even draw up the plans, but the idea had possessed her one night in the wee hours: an intellectual exercise based on Ampère's discoveries about electricity and magnetism. These forces could connect with the spiritual energy that ran through all living things—her prosthetics had proved it over and over. But could the technology be harnessed in such a way as to create a tool that would operate through force of will? She had to know.

Writing it all down had been her mistake.

Her next mistake was not destroying the plans the minute she'd committed them to paper. As soon as Javert had seen them, the project was out of her hands. That had been more than a year ago. She'd run to Hermine. Now Hermine was gone, and as sure as the sun was rising, it wouldn't take long before the finger would point at her. It always did. Any time misfortune confounded weak and superstitious minds, those minds would find someone to blame. And blame liked nothing better than an outsider. A foreigner. A woman with a basement full of tools no one knew how to use, and a mind full of knowledge few people could comprehend.

Thunder cracked through the dawn like gunfire. Outside, the clouds burst open with a wet crash.

Last night's fire had died down to coals, but the coals were still bleeding heat. She crossed to the fireplace and added a handful of kindling. Slowly, gently, she teased the flame back to life. When it was strong enough, she added a few larger pieces of aromatic wood. More expensive than coal, but so much more pleasant.

Too many people were after the plans. She should throw them on the fire right now. But she couldn't bear to. Instead, she would hide them until her bags were packed and she had some idea where to go when she'd left Paris behind. Carefully removing the books from the corners of the long paper, she rolled the plans up and tucked them under her arm. A piece of glass ground under the sole of her slipper as she turned. Last month's issue of *Annales de Chimie* leaned against the broken windowpane near the brick that had broken the window. So much for Hermine's influence protecting her. The minute Maria had left, it seemed the whole city had turned against her.

She found a jar of glue underneath some newspapers, as well as the piece of plain paper in which she'd hidden the plans when she'd liberated them from Javert. Checking the front-door lock, she returned to the attic with these objects, the plans tucked carefully beneath one arm.

Her bedroom was her sanctuary, and she would miss it. A wine-colored Persian carpet lay over the floorboards. It had come with the house, as had the wardrobe that stood on the opposite wall. There was a vanity table—seldom used—and a low chest of drawers. So much storage. Maria had left Romania with the clothes on her back and had—always to Hermine's chagrin—not done much to replace them. Having few possessions made it easy to keep tidy. And to move the wardrobe back from the wall. And to leave when, inevitably, her situation turned against her once more.

She knelt beside the wardrobe and smoothed the plans along the floor before folding the paper into quarters. She laid the plans on the parcel paper, painted glue around the edges of the paper, and pasted it carefully to the back of the wardrobe. Then she pushed the wardrobe into place again. It wasn't perfect, but it would be good enough. An intruder would probably search the lab, the front room, possibly the kitchen. Even if they searched the attic room, it was unlikely they would think to look there.

She twisted the lid back onto the jar of glue and wiped her fingers on the rug. She set the jar of glue onto the vanity table and glanced longingly at her bed, her natural eye burning, her head light from lack of sleep. There was a book on the end table. Perhaps if she just—

She sprang up at the sound of footsteps in front of her house. The sky was just beginning to go gray. It was too early for visitors, too early to even be walking the streets. Her hand went to her robe pocket, where she found a small silk bag with bones and herbs. She rubbed the little bag between her fingers, feeling the delicate twig-like bird bones and the organic brittleness of the herbs. The footsteps shuffled again, and for a moment Maria thought the intruder had changed his mind. The spring-coiled tightness in her stomach eased.

And then came a firm knock upon the door.

❖

Dr. Maria Kalderash lived in a two-story house set into a wall of shops and apartments along the Rue des Rosiers. The area was home to a variety of immigrants and exiles outside the city wall. All in all, a fitting place to find an outcast. Outside, most of the windows were still dark, the doors firmly bolted from within. But later that day, the area would come alive with a hundred different languages, and carts bearing comfort foods from distant homelands would spring up like mushrooms on both sides of the narrow, twisting street.

As Corbeau passed through the gray stone canyon, she was greeted by the familiar sounds of a neighborhood waking: the jangle of keys in a lock, the creak of a window opening overhead, the self-conscious scrabble of the cesspool cleaners as they collected each building's refuse into barrels to transport to the drying yards. A sudden clap of thunder shook the air. Corbeau sighted Dr. Kalderash's door and hurried across the muddy street just as the rain began again. Pressing as close to the house as Javert's umbrella would allow, she rapped on the door. She heard no answer for a moment, then cautious footfall in the hallway. The door cracked open.

"Yes?"

Dr. Kalderash stood no higher than Corbeau's shoulder, but even in the diminished light of the early morning, in the unexpected vulnerability of her dressing gown, her presence filled the doorway. Corbeau's breath caught in her throat. Heat rushed to her cheeks, and she felt the same disorienting sense of awe she had felt when she'd beheld the inventor's picture in Javert's carriage. Dr. Kalderash blinked her natural eye—large and liquid brown—while the mechanical one clicked and whirred as if it, too, was taking Corbeau's measure.

It was a startling combination—a full, pleasingly feminine face, an expression of rightful suspicion, metal, and dark hair cropped shorter than Corbeau had ever seen on a woman. And there was the Eye: a surprisingly elegant nest of gears and lenses attached to a decorated leather band that buckled around the back of the inventor's head. It left Corbeau stumbling for words.

"I have some bread and cheese if you want it," said Kalderash.

"What?"

Kalderash's suspicion had softened to pity, and Corbeau realized what she must have looked like. Her face was battered and swollen. Her coat was soaked, her hems muddy, her hair a straggly, tangled mess.

"If you can sew, I'll have work for you toward the end of the day."

"I'm sorry, there must be some mistake. My name is—"

But suspicion had returned. Kalderash's eyes widened with panic. Corbeau followed her gaze to the insignia pinned to her lapel. "Wait," Corbeau said.

Had the inventor trafficked with the Bureau before? It would have to have been recently, and Vidocq hadn't mentioned it. Corbeau pushed through the door just as Kalderash tried to slam it shut. She grabbed for the inventor's wrist, but Kalderash twisted, gave her a push, and fled down the hall. Tossing the umbrella aside, Corbeau sprang after her. The hallway wasn't more than five long steps. As Kalderash's hand reached for the back doorknob, Corbeau dove. They hit the floor hard, skidded across the worn floorboards, and crashed to a stop against the door in a tangle of hard-muscled limbs, damp skirts, and velvet.

"I just need to speak with you." Corbeau panted as she pulled herself on top of the struggling woman. She twined her legs around the inventor's and held her arms down. Kalderash was strong for her size, and Corbeau had to hold her wrists against the floor so she could catch her breath. Corbeau's pulse raced. The thrill of physical pursuit had been one of the better parts of police work—and her favorite part of affairs. It had been a long time since she'd experienced either. She found the comparison disconcerting. Swallowing hard, she calmed her breathing.

Javert would have considered Kalderash's flight an admission of guilt and hauled her off forthwith. But Corbeau no longer had the authority to make an arrest. Besides, it had seemed that Kalderash had reacted to the Bureau insignia specifically, rather than to the general idea of police.

"My name is Elise Corbeau. I'm a detective inspector of the Sûreté. I've come to ask you a few questions about your acquaintance, Hermine Boucher."

The inventor stopped struggling and stared back up at her, her natural eye wide, the lenses of the mechanical one frantically adjusting and evaluating. Her scars weren't as disfiguring as Javert's description had led Corbeau to believe—just two raised, pinkish lines across tea-colored skin. Her lips were lush and dark. Corbeau became acutely conscious of the soft flesh bruising beneath her fingers, the heart beating rapidly through the velvet robe, and the mingled scents of cinnamon, machine oil, and fear. Corbeau cleared her throat.

"Just a few questions. Please, Doctor." She sat up, slightly embarrassed, and freed the inventor's hands. When Kalderash still didn't move, her embarrassment went from personal to professional. The Paris police had no love for Gypsies. Perhaps Corbeau had misread the situation. Perhaps Kalderash would have run from any government official—especially if she had crossed their paths when she first arrived in Paris. "I'm not going to hurt you." Corbeau rolled off and sat next to her on the floor. "But I'm not leaving without your statement."

Kalderash slowly pulled herself up. She patted her cropped hair into place and adjusted the Eye. Her hands were trembling, but she nodded.

"Is there somewhere we can talk?"

"The front room."

Corbeau rose and brushed herself off. She held out a hand, but Kalderash waved it away and rose slowly to her feet.

Even if Kalderash was innocent, Corbeau thought, as she followed her back down the hall, she had more reason than most to fear the police. The scars that marred her round face—even the blinded eye—might well have been the work of Corbeau's colleagues. Her chin-length hair could have grown out from a shearing, a favorite police method for welcoming Gypsies to Paris. Something else lay behind her hostility as well—something Javert would never understand. It was difficult enough just being a woman, with all the attendant expectations of family, society, and church. But the moment-by-moment grind of being a woman in a man's sphere was enough to make anyone hostile.

The original Sûreté had been a network of reformed criminals like herself. Quite a number of women had been employed as informers. A few, like Corbeau, had specialized knowledge that allowed them to carve out a place for themselves as agents and eventually, in her case, as a detective inspector. But that didn't mean that everyone accepted her presence. From most, grudging tolerance was the best she could expect. Corbeau would have bet money that Kalderash had experienced much the same in the scientific sphere.

As Dr. Kalderash turned in to the front room, Corbeau paused to shut the front door and to pick up Javert's umbrella and lean it against the wall. When she entered the room, Kalderash was on the other side, tending the fire. Glancing up, Kalderash replaced the poker in its rack and shut a lacquered box on the mantel.

"Sit. Please, Inspector." The inventor nodded toward a pair of chairs flanking the fireplace.

The front room had once been outfitted for receiving. A wooden privacy screen stood along the wall opposite the window. Next to it sat a table with implements that could have been either medical or mechanical. Near the doorway was another table with a silver tea urn; Corbeau could hear the soft burbling of the water as it reached a boil. But a long time had passed since either patients or customers had come with any frequency. A guest chair sat abandoned in one corner. An untidy writing desk dominated the front window. The bookcases that lined two of the walls were crammed with books and monographs. Even the surface around the tea urn was losing its fight against stacks of journals, sketches, notes, and metalworking tools.

Corbeau took the proffered chair. It had been expensive once, but the fabric was worn shiny, and the wood had recently met with violence. She watched as Kalderash crossed to the urn and filled two cups with steaming water. She decanted concentrated tea from the pitcher on top of the urn, then set the cups on saucers. Bringing one of the cups to the table at Corbeau's elbow, she pulled another chair near the fire to face her.

"The French are a coffee-drinking people, I know." The doctor had regained some of her composure, but Corbeau could tell she still wasn't happy entertaining her. "But I have so few indulgences anymore. Tea reminds me of home. So you'll allow me this one comfort before you arrest me."

❖

"Arrest you?" the constable asked. Not a constable, Maria reminded herself. A detective inspector. That kind of mistake could cost her a beating, or worse.

"You're here because you believe I had something to do with Hermine's disappearance."

Whether the inspector believed it or not was immaterial. Javert had noticed the missing plans and was marshaling his considerable resources to recover his property, and probably to punish her for good measure. The inspector was wearing the insignia of the Department of the Unexplained, and that meant trouble.

It was a nice touch sending a handsome woman to do the deed, Maria thought. Inspector Corbeau had taken her lumps recently, but beneath the dirt and bruises lay a regal bone structure, strong muscles, and a hint of rather nice curves around the chest and hips. The dress was dreadful, but probably police issue. With a little attention, she would probably be striking. Not pretty, exactly, but attractive, and just Maria's type.

Maria had never discussed her personal life with her colleagues, but considering she was an unmarried female who supported herself with her hands and her brain, assumptions had been made nonetheless. She supposed it was unfair of her to make the same assumptions about the inspector, but it was human nature, was it not?

"Doctor, I fear we've gotten off on the wrong foot. Let's begin again. I'm investigating Madame Boucher's disappearance, but at this point, I'm merely gathering information. You were at the party the other evening, and you had a close connection to the victim. Is there anything you can tell me about that night?"

"I had nothing to do with it. What else do you need to know?"

Slightly mollified, Maria smoothed her robe over her knees and set her china cup on the table beside her. She didn't believe for a moment that the inspector intended to leave without her in shackles. But she could afford to sit in her front room for a bit, sipping tea with a handsome woman until either the inspector left of her own accord or the little spell Maria had worked began to take effect.

The inspector shifted in her seat, unconsciously mirroring Maria's posture, the suggestion of a frown between her eyebrows. For a terrifying instant she thought the inspector must have sensed her defensive charm. But then Corbeau picked up her own tea and sipped, a thoughtful expression on her face, as if she was seriously considering the question.

Corbeau didn't have the smug air of Chief Inspector Vautrin. Maria hadn't seen him for a little over a year after their extended introduction in a back office of the Conciergerie. And then just when she'd thought her days of dealing with French government officials were well behind her, she'd found herself thrust into his company socially. He hadn't seemed to remember her—had he really "interrogated" that many women in that back room that their faces would have blended all together? But him, she would never forget. No, the inspector didn't ooze malice like Vautrin did, but Inspector Corbeau was, like him, a representative of the government and therefore not to be trusted.

Maria fingered the sachet in her pocket. The edges of her eyes began to burn. The herbs she had thrown on the fire were mingling with the smoke. It wouldn't be long now.

"Doctor, let's not play games. A woman to whom you were close has disappeared under mysterious circumstances. At some level, I'm sure you care what happened to her. And you must remember something from that evening."

Maria's hand went unconsciously to the scar that crossed her right cheek. Despite the inspector's reasonable words, the police were rarely better than the criminals they arrested. And yet, as she continued to examine the inspector's face, the calm way she spoke, and the comforting strength in the way she held herself, Maria thought that if she were ever foolish enough to trust an agent of the government, she could do worse than Inspector Corbeau. "It's natural, I suppose, that I would be a suspect after the way we parted."

"Badly?" Corbeau asked.

"In the worst, most public way possible." What a stupid admission. Shaking her head, Maria wondered if the charm she had worked was turning back on her. "But I didn't harm her. I wouldn't. I'm a healer, not a killer, Inspector."

"What did you argue about?"

What hadn't they argued about? In the end, the arguments had always come back to the question of Hermine's spiritual gifts—gifts she had spent most of her life trying to suppress. Maria had begged Hermine to allow her to train those gifts. With the immense power she possessed, Hermine could have changed the world. But Hermine had spent most of her life believing herself cursed. And in the end, it had crushed the fragile happiness that bloomed for such a short time between them. "You might say we had philosophical differences."

Corbeau cocked an eyebrow. "I've only once heard of someone coming to harm over philosophical differences. That was at the university. After talking to the victim's colleagues, I remember being surprised it didn't happen more often."

Kalderash shrugged. "You're wearing the insignia of the Department of the Unexplained. Surely you know quite a bit about philosophical differences."

"Department of the Unexplained?" Corbeau ran a thumb over her pin.

"Or whatever it's called. There must have been times when you knew something out of the ordinary was happening, but a colleague insisted there was a natural explanation."

"There's always a natural explanation."

"Or perhaps you disagreed about the meaning of 'natural.' No doubt the arguments became heated at times, even though an outsider might consider the question to be one of mere semantics."

The inspector pulled at her collar. The whites of her eyes were reddening. The faint sweetness of the herbs was noticeable now amid the aromatic smoke. Maria felt a twinge of guilt. The spell had seemed necessary at the time, when she had wanted to disarm the inspector and get her out as quickly as possible. But now that the conversation had turned from her probable guilt, she was interested to see which direction it would take. Inspector Corbeau coughed.

"I've found that events that people attribute to spirits, when they have no ordinary explanation, often turn out to be manifestations of a force within the individual. Especially in the case of adolescent girls," Corbeau said.

"Girls who are beginning to feel the chains of society's expectations, perhaps?"

"Often, yes. Cases of objects moving by themselves, lamps spontaneously bursting, fires from nowhere—these things inevitably occur, and only occur in the presence of certain individuals. Individuals with repressed anger, frustration, or fear. Which leads me to believe that it's not an outside force perpetrating these events, but some power unconsciously wielded by the individual."

"A natural explanation. That's what I always told Hermine. But she was convinced it was demons and that it was her work here on earth to expel them."

"Was this the real mission of the Church of the Divine Spark?" The inspector set down her cup and turned toward Maria. The chains of magic should have been pulling at her consciousness, dulling her instincts while stirring up a desire to leave. But it seemed to be having as little effect on the inspector as it was on Maria, who had, through regular exposure, become immune. "Were you, Doctor, involved in suppressing supernatural powers—demons, as some call them—as well as providing medical care to the poor?"

Maria's heart pounded. She wasn't prepared for this line of questioning. She didn't know if it would make her a better suspect or a less plausible one. "I have nothing more to say on this subject."

A light in the inspector's eye showed that she knew that Maria had, actually, plenty more to say. Inspector Corbeau sat back in her chair and steepled her fingers beneath her chin. Maria's Eye tingled as the gears and lenses adjusted to her panic. It felt as if the inspector were looking straight through her.

"Then perhaps you could tell me how long you and Madame Boucher were involved."

"A little over two years."

"You don't seem very upset about her disappearance."

"It was a relief, actually." Maria cursed the words that jumped out of her mouth. Each one was another loop on the noose. She scrambled to make her statement sound less damning than it was. "Hermine was an unbalanced woman with a violent temper. She did that," Maria said as the inspector ran an evaluative finger over the deep scratch in the arm of her chair.

"I see. And yet you stayed with her?"

Maria frowned. "I loved her, or at least I did once. And her connections were…useful." Maria declined to continue that it was Hermine's connections that protected her from Javert's wrath once she had left his employ. "I placated her until it was more danger than it was worth. And after I left, her followers turned on me like a pack of rabid dogs."

"Did you go to confront her at the party the other day?" the inspector asked.

"I went to deliver a device the host had ordered. Had I known Hermine would be there, I never would have gone."

"But you did, and you had words with her."

"Yes. We had words. Then I left."

"Before Madame Boucher?"

"Well before her. I assure you, Inspector, I had nothing to do with what happened later."

"If she was violent toward you, no one would blame you for defending yourself."

"I didn't do it!"

"Why did you run earlier when you recognized my insignia?"

Maria's heart raced. She was breathing hard. The inspector, by contrast, looked unperturbed. She fumed when she realized the aggressive turn in the inspector's questioning had probably been an interrogation technique, and it had worked. She smoothed her robe down again and clenched her shaking hands tightly together in her lap. There was no sound but for the clicking of the lenses of her mechanical Eye and the pounding of her pulse in her ears. One of the outer lenses was fogging over. Maria stifled the urge to take the entire apparatus off and polish it with the edge of her robe. "I suppose it does look suspicious," she admitted frostily. "I suppose everyone says I was the last to see her alive."

"No. The last one to see her alive was the footman."

"Lambert?" Maria asked.

The word was like a bolt of lightning from the ceiling. The inspector's eyes went wide and her thin lips gaped open for a split second before she righted herself. Armand Lambert had been one of Maria's only allies among Hermine's people. His information had allowed her to stay one step ahead of Hermine's attacks—attacks Maria had thought would end when Hermine disappeared.

What had happened to him?

"Doctor," the inspector said, "Do the names Claudine Fournier or Michel Bertrand mean anything to you?"

Of course they did. Claudine and Michel had been the only other two of Hermine's entourage who had given her the time of day. Despite the calming herbs now thick in the air, Maria began to panic.

"Inspector, I think you should go."

❖

"No," Corbeau said. She blinked furiously, wiping burning moisture from the corner of one eye, and coughed. The aromatic wood in the fireplace was hiding something else—something sweet and familiar. Something Corbeau was kicking herself for not recognizing immediately. The inventor was working some sort of herb-magic—Corbeau would have bet her left hand on it. But that could wait. She'd stumbled across an important piece of the puzzle, and she wouldn't leave until she'd found where it fit in. She sat back in the chair, crossed her legs, and poised pencil over paper. "Who were they?"

Claudine Fournier was a fire-starter—that was all that Corbeau knew. Not an arsonist—Fournier's fires were never intentional. Rather, they sprang up around her in times of fear, anger, or distress. Corbeau had attended Fournier several days earlier in the Montagne Ste. Geneviève. Like Armand Lambert, Fournier had been causing a disturbance in the rooming house in which she was staying. Corbeau had sedated her with the same pills she had given Lambert, cleaned up the ashes, and left, hoping that whatever upset had been behind the young woman's outburst would be gone by the next morning. When she'd heard nothing, she'd assumed her efforts had been successful.

She'd attended Michel Bertrand a day later, also in the Montagne Ste. Geneviève. Bertrand had heard voices. He also generated them. Not the delusions of a madman, but conversations taking place in other times and venues that were occurring at present or would later occur. That had been one of the more sought-after powers for which people had approached Corbeau when she had been immersed in the criminal life. But like Fournier, Bertrand had desired most deeply to rid himself of what he considered a curse.

"One incident is an anomaly, Doctor. Two could be a coincidence. But three outbursts of supernatural energy in the same area in the same week have to be related. You say Lambert was Madame Boucher's footman. Let me tell you…" She coughed again. A tight, throbbing headache was creeping forward from her temples. "Lambert was one of the last to see her before she disappeared." She remembered Lambert's disheveled state, his meager possessions—so much like Fournier and Bertrand.

And now Vautrin had at least one of them.

The air was stifling. Corbeau glanced toward the hallway. She imagined the cool, moist air that would rush in if she threw the front door open. She breathed it in, feeling the rain on her cheeks, the moisture in her nostrils. As she rose from the chair, she caught herself.

Lambert had been Madame Boucher's footman. Had Fournier and Bertrand worked for her as well? All three of them seemed out of place in the tenements where she'd found them. Respectable people who had experienced a sudden change in circumstance—a change for the worse. They had all been running from something. Perhaps, like Lambert, Bertrand and Fournier had attended Madame Boucher at the time of her disappearance. Why, then, had their names not appeared on Vautrin's report?

Corbeau massaged her temples. The headache had formed a tight band around her skull and was squeezing sharply with each throb. The air felt thick and noxious. It was all she could do to not run from the room. "Tell me what you think of my theory, Doctor."

Kalderash frowned—one thick, dark eyebrow pulling toward the Eye. She raised her head, looking squarely at Corbeau, her lips tight with—could it have been irritation? The device emitted a slow series of clicks. A blue pinpoint of light began to glow behind the nested lenses, and Corbeau's skin crawled. A fireplace log split with a loud crack. That same familiar fragrance rose from the wood—something more than sap, more than the distinct aroma of the tree.

"I think Claudine Fournier and Michel Bertrand also worked for Madame Boucher," Corbeau said. "A paid companion, perhaps, and the driver."

Kalderash shifted in her chair. Corbeau coughed again, but her pulse raced. There was definitely something to the idea. She could feel it. She caught the inventor's natural eye and held it, unblinking. "It…it is as you say," Kalderash finally admitted.

"The three of them were likely the last to see Madame Boucher before she disappeared. You mentioned the victim had a violent temper. How did she treat her employees?" Corbeau ran a fingernail over a jagged gash that ran along the arm of her chair. The gash was fresh, the exposed wood still clean and light.

"Like that chair, we all felt her wrath on occasion."

"Did she give you those scars?"

"No. Those came courtesy of the police."

Corbeau felt a brief pang of shame, but it was eclipsed by anger as she recognized the familiar scent hiding in the smoke. Outrage cut through the clouds beginning to fog the edges of her vision and allowed her to gather up the tendrils of thought that had begun to wander. She laughed mirthlessly under her breath. Clever, clever doctor. But not quite clever enough. She straightened, tucking her pen and paper into her coat pocket. "I see."

"I don't suppose you're about to offer an apology."

"An apology?" Corbeau really did laugh this time. "Tell me, Doctor, did you really think a Bureau agent wouldn't recognize widow's root?"

Kalderash's natural eye blinked. Her plump, perfectly formed lower lip dropped open in amazement. "You know it?"

Of course Corbeau knew it. It was one of the main ingredients in the pills she'd developed while working for Vidocq. "My mother used to throw it on the fire during a difficult childbirth. Or when she needed to bring a troublesome magistrate around to her way of thinking.

"Quite frankly, I had wanted to believe a conspiracy of disgruntled servants had done away with Madame Boucher. It would have been much more plausible than some nonsense about a Gypsy sorceress and her black magic. But your actions this morning tell me there's probably something to the hysteria going around the scandal sheets. If there was a conspiracy, I'm pretty damn sure that you were at the center of it. I'll prove it, in fact." She fixed Kalderash with a smoldering glare. "In the meantime, don't even think of trying to leave the city."

Corbeau stalked to the door, wishing for all the world she could take the woman in without a warrant. She hadn't been convinced of Kalderash's guilt when she'd arrived, but the inventor was a practitioner and hadn't hesitated to use her art against her. She could protest her innocence until Christ returned. As far as Corbeau was concerned, Dr. Maria Kalderash had declared her own guilt.

"Wait!" Kalderash cried as Corbeau reached for the doorknob. The metal was cool, and its touch eased the throbbing in Corbeau's head immediately.

Corbeau didn't wait. She threw the door open. The cold, wet air was a needed slap in the face. She strode toward the sidewalk, pulling her coat tightly around her. The rain beat down, plastering her hair to her head and soaking her to the bone. But she didn't care. She was going straight to the Conciergerie to get the arrest warrant from Javert. Some part of her was disappointed that it hadn't taken even a day's work to conclude that he'd been right. But it didn't matter. She'd have the warrant in her hand by lunchtime. And after that, she'd take Sophie up on her offer of a hot bath and silk sheets.

## CHAPTER SIX

The walk from the Rue des Rosiers to the prefecture headquarters on the Île de la Cité gave Corbeau time for her hands to stop shaking with fury, and her mind to return to a state of reason. She strode along the Seine, crossing a bridge to Paris's administrative center, where she would find the Palais de Justice and, within its stone walls, Prefect Claude Javert.

As she walked up the Boulevard du Palais, the Conciergerie clock struck one. Corbeau was used to hearing its doleful toll, but rarely when she was passing directly in front of it. The clock at Notre Dame struck the hour a split second after. The combined sound shook the air around her and rattled her bones. Symbolic, she thought, of the position of the late Bureau of Supernatural Investigations—the position occupied only by herself, now—that hard place between the demands of justice and the requirements of the Church.

Hugging her shoulder bag close to her side, she blew on her hands and shoved them into her coat pockets. It had been a long time since she had allowed a suspect to rattle her like Kalderash had. It was more than the insult of widow's root—such a transparent trick. And it was more than the sting of realizing she hadn't figured out what Kalderash was doing until it was almost too late.

Under different circumstances, she would have found a lot to admire in Kalderash. She had to be incredibly tough, for one thing. To have found a way to rise from her circumstances, educate herself, and make her way to Paris would have been difficult enough had Kalderash been a man. Being a woman added an entirely new layer of opposition, which alone would have worn all but the hardiest of souls down. And to find herself in Paris, and to stay despite all of the city's best attempts to drive her away—it boggled the mind.

And there was her work. Kalderash was best known for her toys, but Corbeau suspected that the Gin Liver and Stomach Bypass had merely been a means to a financial end. Dr. Kalderash's home had the untidy look of someone who lived and breathed research. What was Kalderash working on now? The mess suggested it was something all-consuming. Of course Kalderash wouldn't have taken an agent of the la Sûreté into the heart of her research. She had to have a workshop somewhere. Corbeau would have given her eyeteeth to see it.

Finally, there was no denying that, under other circumstances, Corbeau would have found Kalderash attractive. It was a strange and disconcerting sensation, and the feelings that it had stirred up—feelings she'd thought long behind her—were both exciting and panic-inducing. Images and impressions flashed through her mind: the Eye, which made the inventor seem simultaneously imposing and frail; soft flesh beneath her fingertips as she'd held Kalderash to the floor; the inventor's own curious blend of sweet and mechanical scents; the dry, choking smoke, which even still filled her nostrils.

It was a shame the inventor was guilty and that the only satisfaction Corbeau would gain would be to see her in a prison cell.

Corbeau's chest tightened as she approached the Palais de Justice. She had been to the building once or twice, but Vidocq had always had his agents out in the field. Even after being promoted to detective inspector, Corbeau wasted precious little time in those lofty halls. It was only after Vautrin had clipped her wings that Corbeau had spent more time indoors than out—and that had been at the local office.

The bleak, brown walls of the former palace loomed over a long courtyard that sat some twelve feet below street level. It was an imposing fortress on the outside. Inside, one wing housed a labyrinth of offices belonging to the prefecture and shadowy groups vaguely affiliated with the Ministry of the Interior. The other wing of the building contained the Conciergerie, the prison. During the great revolution, the Conciergerie had housed over one thousand prisoners plus the revolutionary tribunal. Now only the most infamous prisoners were kept within the cells. Corbeau wondered whether Kalderash's crimes would earn her a place there.

Corbeau's hands began trembling again. It was silly to be intimidated by this place of mere stone and suggestion. Especially considering that the prefect of police himself had hired her to do exactly what she was doing. But she wasn't unaware of her position as a decommissioned police inspector, as the last remaining member of a bureau disbanded with prejudice. And she wasn't unaware that she looked like something dredged up from the bottom of the Seine. Taking a deep breath and forcing her thoughts to still, she ran a hand through her hair. She brushed off her face with the sleeve of her coat and smoothed the coat down over the dress that she would toss onto the fire at the nearest possible opportunity. Then she began to walk to the entrance.

As she approached the gate, she was relieved to see a familiar face. "Laveau, it's good to see you," she said to the guard.

As he recognized her, an easy smile spread across his face. "Inspector, as I live and breathe." Laveau was several years younger than she was. He'd been one of the Bureau's last hires and had held his job an entire three months before Vautrin had given him the sack.

"You look well," Corbeau said. "The uniform suits you."

Laveau brushed an imaginary speck from the thick wool coat that covered his stout form most impressively. The hat that covered his well-tended dark hair looked warm. "I thought you were long gone."

"I would have been, if Vautrin had had his way."

At the mention of the chief inspector, Laveau's expression turned sour. "You must have friends in high places."

"For better or for worse," Corbeau said. "That's what brings me here, actually. I've come on the prefect's business."

Laveau gave a low whistle. "Better you than me. Is he expecting you?"

"Eventually."

"Right through those doors." Laveau gestured with his heavy head. "Abandon hope all ye who enter," he said under his breath as Corbeau walked toward them.

The complex that housed the Palais de Justice had been built as a royal residence. Though it hadn't been used that way for over a hundred years, the building still commanded respect and awe. The doors opened up onto a high-ceilinged entryway lit by tall windows. At the point where the entryway narrowed into a long corridor, a stern-featured gatekeeper sat at a long desk. The desk was empty save for a ledger where the fortunate ones granted entrance would sign their names. Though Corbeau and the gatekeeper were the only ones in the vast hall, the air vibrated with the low hubbub of voices behind the closed doors that opened onto either side of the corridor. One couldn't help but feel small in such an environment, and Corbeau was certain that this was, to some degree, the point.

She cleared her throat.

"Inspector Elise Corbeau for Prefect Javert."

The gatekeeper was of similar build to Laveau, but of a soft composition that betrayed the fact that he spent as much time sitting in his chair as Laveau did walking back and forth in front of the Conciergerie doors. As Corbeau approached the desk, he looked up from the scandal sheet he was perusing. "I wasn't aware that the prefect had an appointment at this time."

"I don't have an appointment. But I guarantee he'll want to see me." The gatekeeper scrutinized her with a hardened eye. "Corbeau. Detective Inspector," she repeated.

The officer pursed his lips and looked away, clearly searching for an excuse not to leave his chair. As Corbeau opened her mouth to speak again, a door opened in the back corridor. She held her breath as the familiar form of Chief Inspector Vautrin stepped out into the hallway. Corbeau froze. The bruises his fingers had raised around her neck throbbed dully. She wanted to duck back out the door, but the movement would only catch his attention.

What was he doing here, this morning of all mornings?

Granted, Vautrin had more right to be here than she did. Although he commanded the local office, his administrative duties brought him to the Palais often. Probably more often, now that he was currying the favor of the Church and King. All the same, the memory of their encounter earlier sent a cold shiver through her bowels. Her hand went instinctively to her neck, where his baton had, not twelve hours before, pinned it to the wall. As she willed him to keep moving, he stopped as if sensing a disturbance in the ether. Slowly he turned. His face filled with fury as he recognized her.

"What are you doing here, Madame?"

"I'm here on the prefect's business."

"Your business is what I say it is." A cunning expression crossed his face. "Which reminds me, you didn't report to work this morning."

"You know very well why."

The sharp edges of his mouth turned up. "I do. And I have to say, if your side projects are going to interfere with your job, I don't think even the prefect can justify keeping you on."

Corbeau's headache was returning. Her pulse pounded in her ears. She was there at the behest of Javert himself. Even if Vautrin fired her, Javert would still keep paying her. Wouldn't he? She forced herself to remain calm. "Where's Lambert?" The struck-by-lightning look on his face was almost worth what came next.

"Armand Lambert," she said, turning to the gatekeeper, who had been watching their argument as if it were a game of tennis. "Footman to Hermine Boucher, the sordid details of whose kidnapping are plastered all over the front page of your newspaper, there. Lambert was one of the last ones to see Madame Boucher before she disappeared, which makes him a vital witness in the prefect's investigation." She caught the gatekeeper's eye and pointed to Vautrin. "He was last seen in this man's company."

"Get out," Vautrin said.

"What have you done with him, Chief Inspector? Is he being held next door for the crime of having a nightmare?"

"Get her out of here!"

"Or perhaps your priest could tell me."

Vautrin's face went purple with rage.

Corbeau's mouth went dry as she realized she had pushed too far. Not only did she have no idea what was going on in the Montagne Ste. Genevieve, but whatever was happening, Vautrin had his greasy, sticky fingers all over it. And she had gone against everything Vidocq had taught her and tipped her hand before she had all the facts. But she'd made her bed. The worst thing she could do now would be to back down. "Where's Lambert?" she asked again.

Vautrin tensed forward then caught himself. If the building hadn't been filled with their superiors, Vautrin would have gone for her throat right there and then. A door opened in the corridor, the sound echoing off the high stone walls as some bureaucrat poked his head out to see what the commotion was about.

"I am Inspector Elise Corbeau," Corbeau said, raising her voice so that anyone who was interested could hear clearly. "I'm on an assignment for Prefect Javert. Chief Inspector Vautrin is concealing—"

"You are nobody!" thundered Vautrin. His words filled the high chamber. "I allowed you to pour my coffee and clean the offices as a favor to the prefect, but you didn't show up to do even that this morning! As of this moment, you are no longer employed by the Sûreté. She does not belong here! Guard, see her out!"

The gatekeeper's head bobbed back toward her. "Madame—"

"I'm here at the request of the prefect. I need to see Prefect Javert."

"Escort her out, or you'll be scrubbing chamber pots in the Conciergerie for what's left of your miserable career!"

"I'm sorry, Madame."

The man rose from his desk. Only then did Corbeau witness the magnitude of his physique. He was both tall and wide, and as he straightened, she saw the suggestion of a one-time fighter's formidable musculature. The multiple bruises, insults, and injuries of the morning suddenly clamored for her attention all at once. If it had been one of these men, she might have forced her way in on a good day. But not both of them. Not today. She would have to find a different way to get to Javert.

Vautrin crossed his arms over his chest, a smug expression on his face.

"This isn't over," she said, looking Vautrin in the eye.

He oozed self-satisfaction. For now, at least, he had won. He nodded with mock benevolence. "Good day, Madame."

❖

Outside, the clouds had gathered overhead, dark and portentous. Lightning screamed across the sky, thunder rumbling in its wake. As the heavy doors of the Conciergerie slammed shut behind Corbeau, heavy raindrops began to pelt down from above.

Now what was she supposed to do? She had completed Javert's task—the task that would have seen her reinstated—quicker than he could have hoped, but she had no way of relaying this fact to him. She hugged her shoulder bag close under her arm and pulled her coat tighter around her, stepping back as a passing carriage sprayed the curb with filthy water. If that wasn't enough, she'd left Javert's umbrella in Dr. Kalderash's entryway. She wouldn't be going back there any time soon—not without an arrest warrant in hand. She pushed her hands into her coat pockets and felt the comforting lump of the purse that Javert had passed her that morning. She'd given Marie a few coins, but more than enough remained to have a bite to eat at the café across the street. In fact, if she wanted to, she could sit there all day, waiting for the prefect to emerge. And while she did so, she could review his notes again and compare them to her own. Yes, that's exactly what she would do. She jumped as a light hand settled on her shoulder.

"We have to stop bumping into each other like this, Elise."

Corbeau turned, her irritation melting away as she took in the only friendly face that had greeted her today.

"You are following me."

"Nonsense." Sophie smiled back. She had acquired a fur-lined hat that matched her coat. As she moved closer, Corbeau instinctively relieved her of her ivory-handled umbrella and angled the oiled silk to protect them both. "All the best gossip comes from this part of town."

"Only if you're selling police gossip. You usually prefer society stuff. Tales of the rich and vapid. Interesting, coming from a socialist."

"I'm exposing the upper classes for what they are."

"You're gathering admirers and feathering your nest. Nicely, too, I might add." Corbeau fingered the fur trim of the other woman's hat.

"Still waiting for you to drop by like you promised."

"I didn't promise." Corbeau thought better of it. Kalderash wasn't going anywhere, and Javert hadn't expected her to finish her investigation this early anyway. Her entire body felt suddenly heavy. Her head pounded, and she could feel—acutely—every scratch, bruise, cut, and ding that she had sustained since foolishly stopping at Oubliette for a bottle of wine after work the previous day. Sophie was still looking at her expectantly. Corbeau shook her head. "I'd be honored," she said.

Sophie beamed and held up a manicured hand. A well-appointed fiacre seemed to materialize out of nowhere, its fresh paint gleaming through the rain, the horse healthy and neatly turned out. One look at Sophie, and the driver hopped down from his perch and opened the door for them. Corbeau was surprised he didn't lay his coat across the puddle between the curb and the carriage step. She felt a twinge of jealousy as the driver took Sophie's delicate hand in his and assisted her up. It didn't help that when he was done, he began to shut the carriage door behind her.

"Excuse me," Corbeau said.

He glared at her over her shoulder but, after a giggled word from Sophie, stepped back with a bow.

But he didn't offer to help her inside.

Corbeau slid inside, feeling a little self-conscious about her filthy dress on the crisp new leather. But Sophie took her hand and she felt she was exactly where she belonged—at least for now.

## CHAPTER SEVEN

Maria stood in the doorway for some time watching Inspector Corbeau disappear into the early morning Rue des Rosiers bustle and punishing herself with regret. She'd made a terrible mistake. Not only had she underestimated Corbeau's knowledge of herb-magic, but she'd also driven off a potential ally. She was still certain Javert had sent Corbeau, tasked with her arrest. But in retrospect, the inspector had acted as if she was open to other explanations for Hermine's disappearance. She'd been trying to see all the possibilities. And now Maria had not only insulted her intelligence and training, but enraged her by drawing up a spell to ward her off. Inspector Corbeau might have been considering a number of theories to explain what happened to Hermine, but by the time she stormed off, that number had narrowed to one—the exact one that would land Maria right where Javert wanted her.

The inspector had warned her not to leave Paris. She'd probably sent out guards as soon as she arrived back at the Conciergerie. If Maria ran, every agent in Paris would be looking for her. But what other choice did she have?

She shut the door. Turning, she nearly tripped over the inspector's heavy umbrella. The hulking mass of oiled silk and baleen hadn't been designed with a woman in mind, but it suited the inspector perfectly. She ran a finger over the carved handle, and unbidden sensations flooded her mind: the inspector's callused hand with its fine, tapered fingers—held out in apology after she'd knocked Maria down. Maria had wanted to take it, to feel the hard muscles beneath the cool skin—but pride had prevented that. There had been a spark of recognition in the inspector's eye when their conversation had veered into theories of supernatural phenomena. She was an intelligent woman, and experience had made her knowledgeable as well. And she hadn't shied away from Maria's scars, shorn hair, or her Eye. Maria slumped back against the doorway of her cluttered front room and let out a long breath. She'd spent so many years among untrustworthy people that she wouldn't know honest if it walked up and bit her.

And she longed for honest. As far back as she could remember, relationships had always been an exchange of obligation. She bartered the skills she'd learned from her mother and aunts for money—spells and healing exchanged for coin in the dead of night. With money she bought herself out of the slavery in which most Roma still lived in her country. Money bought education as well and, later, medical training. She would have loved to remain in that jewel of a village she'd eventually settled in, attending the needs of both people and machines. But when disease had ravaged the village, her friends and neighbors had wasted no time declaring her a witch and driving her out at the pointed tips of the very tools she'd created for them.

Her correspondence with Claude Javert—the new prefect of the Paris police, and himself a tinkerer—had been a godsend then. He'd brought her to Paris to work in his new organization. Of course everyone knew how that had turned out. When Maria and Javert had fallen out, Hermine had been there to catch her. Hermine had pledged her love, and Maria had lowered her guard. But in the end, as always, the relationship came down to a cold-hearted exchange. From the moment Maria had made the mistake of mentioning the Left Hand of Justice, Hermine had no longer been content with their clinic. She had embarked on a crusade to "cure" all spiritual afflictions, whether or not the "afflicted" wanted to be cured. Hermine's temper, she might have withstood. But this new ambition had hastened the end.

And what, Maria wondered, would Corbeau have wanted from her, when all was said and done?

Thunder shook the air, and the clouds threw down a wall of rain. Maria shivered and returned to the front room. Too little water was left in the samovar to bother with, so she removed the teapot from the top and let the coal smolder. The fire crackled away in the fireplace, the dried widow's root she had thrown onto the logs now just a trace of sweetness in the air. She fished a monograph on mathematics out of the pile on her desk. Just as she was about to sit down, a shadow flashed against the front-window curtain. She drew the curtain back, gasping as a bird—a mass of black-and-white feathers, wild eyes luminous with reflected lamplight, hurled itself against the glass. The bird hit hard and slid down, and Maria heard it thump quietly to the ground outside.

Her grandmother had taught her a magpie was a message: quarrel and strife. As if she needed a sign to tell her that. More importantly, her research had forced her to recognize the spark of the divine—the Spirit, if you will—present in all living organisms, whether fish or bird or tree or even prefect of police. A thrumming, crackling field of spirit surrounded each and every living thing, which meant that it would be evil to simply let this creature drown in a puddle outside her window.

Dropping the magazine, Maria hurried out into the rain, crouched on the wet pavement, and gathered it up in the folds of her robe.

"Oh, you poor thing."

The bird safe in her hands, she hurried back inside. Wiping her bare feet, now pale with cold, on the rough mat just inside the entrance, she locked the door behind her. Then she reached up to the wainscoting on the adjacent wall and withdrew a key. The small doorway in the corridor had originally served to connect the servants' area with the upstairs. Maria had no use for servants. They were an expense and a liability. But the basement made an ideal laboratory.

The bird trembled in her hand. As she paused on the staircase, it stared up at her with a dazed expression, its neck at a disconcerting angle. It would not live. But it had served its purpose—it was a message, she was sure of it. All that remained was to decode it. The poor creature would not spend its last moments in fear, wetness, and cold. She paused at the bottom of the staircase to light the gas sconce.

Long tables stood at right angles against the two far walls. Piles of cogs, gears, springs, tools, fabric, and notes marked ideas under development. Such good ideas. Her eyes burned at the thought that this was as far as they might get before she'd be forced to start over. Or would she bother this time? Chill radiated from the basement walls. Laying the bird down on the edge of one of the tables, she lit the brazier in the corner. If she were to work that day, she'd need warmth.

After she tucked the tinderbox back in its place, she found a square of blue silk, shook it out, and spread it on the table. Gently, she laid the bird on top of it.

Hermine had begged her to find a cure for what she called her affliction. A kinder term, perhaps, than demonic possession, but just as inaccurate. The fact was that Hermine possessed untrained spiritual abilities, the likes of which Maria had never before seen. But in two years, try as Maria might, she had never been able to convince Hermine she was anything but cursed. In retrospect, perhaps Maria should have been more patient. It wasn't her, after all, who had been beset from childhood with unwanted visions. Maria had never moved objects with mere thought. To have been raised in a society where such things were considered signs of indwelt evil—or at least of mental instability—must have been terrifying. Maria wondered whether part of her attraction to Hermine hadn't been the desire for some of Hermine's immense power to somehow rub off on her. That was definitely an aspect of her extraordinary charisma, whether her followers knew it or not.

All the same, Hermine's constant demands that Maria search for a way to suppress her abilities made Maria—who hadn't a gram of inherent spiritual talent—burn with rage. If only Hermine had been more patient, they could have found a way to control her talent together. Hermine might have seen it for the gift that it was.

But Maria had been impatient as well, and she had been jealous. And now things had gone horribly wrong.

The bird shivered on the silk square in front of her. She stroked its head with her finger.

"Who sent you?" she asked. As if she could have understood the answer. Maria hadn't the power to communicate with animals, though Michel Bertrand had.

The bird twitched toward her voice, but its eyes were going unfocused and it labored to breathe. She watched the light in its eyes slowly fade until the eyes were as lifeless as glass and the rise and fall of its chest had stilled. As she stroked its soft stomach, she noticed a small, hard protuberance. And therein lay the message. She was certain of it.

She jumped as someone rapped sharply on the street-level window. She had obscured the window with a thick curtain when she'd first moved in. Only a few people knew that, more often than not, the mistress of the house herself was to be found there. Who was it? What could they want?

"Doctor!"

At the sound of the boy Joseph's voice, she let out a breath of relief. She had no messages for him to run—her network of acquaintances had been turning against her with frightening predictability—but fussing over him would be a welcome distraction.

"Come to the front door," she called.

With a backward glance at the magpie, she climbed the stairs to let him in. Only after he had shut the door behind himself and hung his thin coat on the hook in her vestibule, did she realize that, for the first time, she hadn't heard the unique shuffle of the wooden post he used to walk on. He was using the leg she had crafted confidently and, apparently, comfortably. The graft of the mechanical device to his vital spiritual field had worked even better than she had hoped. The experiment had paid off for them both.

"The apparatus is working well, I see." Of course it was. The device was well made, and the child was brimming with life force.

The boy grinned back. "Better than the one God gave me. If I had two of 'em, I bet I could fly. It's a joke," he said quickly, as Maria felt her expression go hard.

At the height of her devices' popularity, several people had approached her about replacing perfectly healthy limbs with all sorts of terrible things. A few had even drawn up plans. In a way it had been a blessing when Hermine had declared the trend finished. Healing a defect was one thing, but replacing the perfect with the mechanical was an abomination.

"Come downstairs," she said. "I have something to show you."

He followed her to the basement—quietly, nimbly—and emerged just in front of her into the softly lit laboratory. She led him to the table, where the magpie lay, cooling and still.

"What is it?" Joseph asked.

"It's a sign."

"What does it mean?"

"You're going to help me find out. Turn your back just a minute while I put on my work clothes."

Suitably attired, she cleared a spot next to an iron torso cage and pulled up a stool for him. She took his small, thin hand and ran his index finger over the bird's underside, pausing at the hard lump. "Do you feel that?" she asked.

"The breastbone?"

"A bird's bones are hollow, delicate." She pressed his finger down. "Here's the breastbone. Feel how it gives way under pressure?"

"Feels like it swallowed something, then," he said.

"But whatever it is, it's too big for the bird to have swallowed it intact. Hand me a scalpel."

Joseph selected a small one from the towel where she had laid out a selection of cutting tools. Maria fingered the protuberance again. Murmuring apologies to the bird's departed spirit, she took the scalpel in her deft fingers and slit the carcass from throat to vent. She folded back the thin skin from the incision. Metal glinted between the liver and the gizzard. Gingerly, she worked it out and wiped it clean on the sky-blue silk.

"It's Romani magic. This is a bridle ornament." Like the one she carried in her pocket-charm. "We're great horsemen, you know." Her family had been metalsmiths but had shared the Roma people's affinity for horses. She missed the animals' smell, the feel of their muscles beneath her fingers. "Look, these are symbols I learned when I was about your age. Power," she said, pointing to the image of a sun engraved on the surface of the disk. Inside it were inscribed two crescent moons. "And double protection."

"Protection from what?"

She blew out a long breath. A long list of possibilities scrolled through her mind, none more comforting than the others. *Romanian authorities? The Church of the Divine Spark? Monsieur le Préfet? His Holiness the Pope? The Fickle Hand of Fate?*

She shrugged.

"Enemies are everywhere. Take your choice."

"Who put it there?"

She frowned. The sign was one her grandmother had spoken of, though Maria had never seen it before. But everyone she had known in her home country had scattered a long time ago. The only Romani she currently knew was…

"Armand."

"Monsieur Lambert?"

She nodded.

Armand Lambert was her only remaining ally in Hermine's circle. His mother had been Romani; Maria had known it the moment she met him. The fact had bound them on a spiritual level from the start.

"Something's happened to him," she said. She had gained that much from her conversation with Inspector Corbeau. He must have set the sign to manifest in case some evil overtook him. "But it's a strange message, if that's the case."

"He had an attack this morning, Doctor. Just like Mademoiselle Fournier and Monsieur Bertrand. He's gone, now. Vautrin took him. A priest was there as well."

Maria inhaled sharply. Her heart pounded. For Joseph's own protection, she had tried to keep him ignorant of what transpired between her and Hermine. But he was as intelligent as he was useful. Surely he must have begun to sense a connection among the three servants, even if he was unable to articulate the nature of that connection. She hoped, for his sake, that he hadn't realized Vautrin was more than just the chief inspector of the Sûreté. "Mademoiselle Fournier and Monsieur Bertrand, did Vautrin take them as well?" she asked.

"Nobody knows. No one's seen them since last night."

Maria rolled the silver disk between her fingers, catching the gentle light of the wall sconce. First Hermine's lady's maid, the driver, and now the footman—Vautrin was picking off her allies one by one. But the loss of Armand hurt the most. He had been the closest to Hermine. His assistance had helped Maria keep one step ahead of the Church of the Divine Spark, of Vautrin himself, who had sworn himself to her destruction. And now Armand was gone. And yet this sign—power and double protection, even in this most precarious situation—it was not yet time to lose hope.

She pushed a section of hair behind her ear. "Tell me what you think, Joseph. The situation worsens by the minute, and yet, despite the torment to which Vautrin and his priest must be putting him, Armand sends a message of hope. See here? The twin moons in the protective embrace of the sun. Claudine and Michel, perhaps? Or Armand and myself? My question, who is the protector?"

He blinked at her, his eyes, even in the gloom, clear and dancing with intelligence. "There was someone else this morning." The lenses of her mechanical eye turned and clicked into place, as they often did when her mind was reaching unconscious conclusions it would later reveal. She had long ceased to be bothered by the sound but wondered what others must have thought. Joseph spoke more confidently, as if encouraged by it. "Inspector Corbeau of the Sûreté."

Her eye whirred as she focused on his thin face. Her cheeks felt hot, and her pulse pounded.

"You know this person?"

"She was responsible for this," he said, giving his bad leg a shake. "Then later she saved my life. You can trust her. The chief inspector tried to strangle her this morning."

Maria felt a smile tug at the edge of her lips. She'd like to have seen the injuries Vautrin had taken away from the encounter. She had definitely misjudged Elise Corbeau. It wouldn't be the first time fear had blinded her to possible sources of help. Would she have the chance to make it up to the inspector—to show she herself was worthy of trust as well? "You saw that? With Vautrin?"

"I was the one who took her there, to the Montagne Ste. Geneviève. And to see Mademoiselle Fournier and Monsieur Bertrand as well. I thought she could help them. She tried, but I don't think she's ever seen anything like this before."

"Before?"

The boy excitedly related tale after tale of Corbeau's heroic deeds with the Bureau of Supernatural Investigations—a bureau Vautrin had recently disbanded. Maria's mind flashed back to the insignia Inspector Corbeau had worn on her collar—the bell, book, and candle. The insignia had been so similar to the one Javert's Department of the Unexplained had used—no one could blame her for having confused them. The insignia had made her certain Corbeau was working for Javert. Could she have been wrong? She polished the silver disk with her thumb. *Double protection.* Inspector Corbeau would make a very powerful protector.

If only she weren't convinced Maria had kidnapped Hermine Boucher.

"She was here earlier," Maria told the boy. "I sent her away." She sighed and sank down onto the stool. "Javert will never let me be. Not as long as I have what he needs. He must be getting desperate now if he thinks his only option is to frame me for whatever it is that happened to Hermine."

An enormous clap of thunder shook the building. Maria glanced at the amulet again. Running her thumbnail over the engravings—the metal tingled with magic beneath her skin—she tucked it into the inner breast pocket of her robe. It was a small thing, this mysterious hope, and she would have to think more about what it meant. But at this point it was all she had.

"Perhaps Monsieur Javert is your protector," Joseph said. "He was once before. Was he really so bad?"

She thought about it. "He wasn't, not on a personal level. But in the end he wanted the same thing everyone else did. And I couldn't give it to him. Come."

She folded the corners of the silk square around the magpie and slipped it into her pocket. She would lay it on the fire upstairs and let its body follow its spirit into oblivion.

She ushered Joseph up the stairs ahead of her, leaving the wall sconces and the brazier burning. It was time to start work again, and Joseph would soon be on his way. She really had thought things would be better in Paris, away from the small-minded villagers and ingrained superstitions. So many people in Paris, and so many ideas—and yet even in the heart of the modern, enlightened world, she was still a foreigner. If she were still alive in a year's time, it would be interesting to see where she would find herself.

"Is this your umbrella, Doctor?" Joseph asked, as she shut the door to the laboratory behind her.

"It's hers. What do you think? Should I walk it over to the Palais de Justice myself?"

Making her way into the front room, she took the blue silk bundle from her pocket. She cleared a spot in the fire and laid the magpie atop one of the logs. Flames leaped eagerly toward the cuffs of her robe. She snatched her hand away, watching as the flame turned its attention to the silk. She took a pinch of dried herbs from a jar on the mantel and sprinkled it on top.

"Joseph!" she called. She wanted to explain to him what she was doing. He'd shown interest in her mechanical work, but if she was going to pass some of her knowledge to him before she left, he would have to understand some of the spiritual underpinnings. Why hadn't he joined her yet? Was he still fiddling around with that blasted umbrella? "Joseph!"

"Doctor!" he cried.

She whirled at the panic in his voice. She opened her mouth to shout, but her cry was drowned by the sound of splintering wood and shattering glass.

## CHAPTER EIGHT

The elegant set of rooms Sophie kept on Rue St. Dominique hadn't changed, though the benefactors that paid for them seemed to turn with the seasons. The thought of living at someone else's sufferance curdled Corbeau's stomach, but the life seemed to suit Sophie fine. Her quarters were superior in comfort, design, and water-tightness. She never lacked the basics, as Corbeau sometimes did. And it seemed to be a point of pride for Sophie's benefactors that their ornament be well fed and dressed. A nice arrangement, if you could find it. And one with which Corbeau had never been able to compete.

The rain began to fall again, washing the even pavement clean. Beneath the steely skies, the granite facades of the shops seemed to gleam, set off by the black ironwork that marked the apartment windows above. Fashionable people hurried past as Corbeau stepped from the fiacre, slowing to watch Sophie light in the carriage doorway before accepting Corbeau's hand onto the sidewalk. Jealousy sparked in Corbeau's chest as she watched them undress Sophie with their eyes. She snuffed it immediately. Too much time had passed, too much water gone under the bridge for her to have any right to be jealous. Sophie led on, and Corbeau followed her through an unmarked doorway next to a jeweler's shop and up two flights of stairs.

Only a month had passed since Corbeau's last visit, yet Corbeau felt as if she were returning to a place she'd not seen in years. The dark-green door seemed smaller and more brittle. The brass numbers and knob looked the same, yet somehow unfamiliar. Sophie tickled the brass lock with her key, and the door slid open silently across polished wood—just as silently as when Corbeau had stolen away, nearly a month ago to the day, leaving Sophie sleeping safe in her overstuffed bed. The same bold paintings dotted the walls. Whatever dust had been allowed to settle on the crimson molding had been whisked away, probably that morning, by a well-paid hand.

Sophie sloughed off her coat and boots then crossed the room to stoke the coals. A large kettle hung from a hook in the fireplace. Corbeau watched as she checked the water level and resettled the vessel on a stand straddling the coals. Her movements were strong and efficient. She might carry herself like a delicate flower, but there had been a time when she'd been accustomed to hard work. She'd been an invaluable assistant, when Moreau the Alchemist had more work than she was physically capable of performing. Sophie had never had a head for compounding, but she could follow a recipe with precision. And where Corbeau even still risked offending entire rooms every time she opened her mouth, silver-tongued Sophie couldn't turn a corner without turning up new clients as well.

Tension gradually began to drain from Corbeau's neck and back. She hung her coat on the rack near the door and took off her boots. Sophie hadn't been joking—she really was going to set up a bath, right in the middle of her main room. It had been so long since Corbeau had done more than run a moist cloth over her body. The thought of availing herself of a basin of hot water and Sophie's collection of scented soaps made her almost giddy.

Sophie pulled a fine mesh screen halfway across the fireplace, taking care not to damage the hammered-metal dragonflies that adorned it. She laid a sheet across the tiles in front of the fireplace and set a large washing basin on top of it. The basin was strictly for bathing—Sophie sent her linens out. Often. While the kettle warmed over the coals, she poured cold water into the basin and laid out a selection of oils, ointments, and clean, dry cloths. She dripped fragrant oil into the basin, attending to her preparations as if they were sacraments.

What they were about to do was an offense to most Parisians' religious sensibilities as well as to simple common sense—and not merely because they would surely end up behind the lacquered door of Sophie's bedroom. Decent people, when forced to remove the layer of grime that many considered to have divine disease-repelling powers, dabbed themselves off quickly and changed their linen undergarments. Only the decadent ever immersed themselves, never mind with the indulgence of oils, hot water, and someone fetching to apply them.

"What a den of sin," Corbeau said. Her voice broke the tension. "Vanity, sensuality, lust, and we're both still fully dressed. Can't wait for Vautrin to read my proof of confession for this one."

"You forgot pleasure. It's not technically a sin, even though people think it should be."

"Since when do you believe in sin?"

"I've been making a study."

Corbeau peeled off her wet socks and stuffed them into her boots. She squatted, resting her elbows on her knees. Of all the changes they'd gone through during their separation, she'd never expected Sophie would flirt with religion. And what a funny kind of religion—so blasé about the carnal transgressions that were about to transpire, yet so earnest about the existence of actual spiritual wrongdoing.

What would qualify as a sin in the Church of the Divine Spark? The King's courting of the nobility at the expense of the poor would probably be high on the list. Unlike Madame Boucher's group, the King didn't have much interest in soothing the fevered brows of slum-dwellers. Corbeau had met a few people like Boucher when she had been a slum-child: women, mostly, who were bored with their riches, but who inexplicably found fulfillment ladling out thin porridge in the back rooms of churches or trying to teach feral, lice-bitten urchins to read the Bible. At least Corbeau had assumed it made them happy; otherwise why would they have bothered?

In retrospect, Corbeau figured the wealth and ease in which these women lived gave them the time to wonder about the meaning of their lives. Perhaps they recognized the fundamental emptiness of the endless rounds of parties and new dresses that their charges in the slums dreamed of. Perhaps they wished for their lives to amount to something more. What was the point, Corbeau wondered, at which money became more of a burden than it was worth? Perhaps one day she would know. But it wouldn't be any time soon.

Corbeau looked around Sophie's well-appointed rooms. They had both come from the same mean streets. Sophie had figured out early how to trade on her looks and companionship, and Corbeau, on her brains and bravado. Corbeau had found fulfillment in work. As for Sophie, the luxury in which she now lived was more than either of them could have imagined as children. Had she started to think about the meaning of it all? Was this why she was so enamored with Madame Boucher's slum crusade?

"Soph?"

"Mmm?"

"Just how involved are you with the Church of the Divine Spark?"

Sophie added a final bowl of boiling water to the cold water in the basin and set the bowl on the floor next to the fireplace. "Elise," she said, hand on hip, tone full of mock irritation, "do you ever stop talking about work?" She smiled devilishly. "Now take off that dress. It's filthy."

The deflection attempt was transparent, but Corbeau let it go. She had to remind herself that the blunt approach wasn't always best with subtle creatures. Moreover, she couldn't stop herself from glancing down at her bedraggled dress. The wool skirt was heavy with water, the hems black with the multitude of unsavory things she had walked through that morning. The nightshirt she had thrown it over was likewise soaked through. The thought of laying any of it over one of Sophie's silk-covered chairs, or hanging it on the coatrack next to Sophie's expensive coat, mortified her. No doubt sensing her thoughts, Sophie laughed.

"Just leave it on the floor, Elise." Corbeau returned her smile nervously. For more reasons than one, she couldn't get the dress off fast enough. "I'll have that nightshirt mended for you," Sophie added, glancing at the garments pooled at Corbeau's feet. "Poor thing. You're as pathetic as an old bachelor. Come here."

Corbeau stepped out of the pile of cold, damp clothing. There was no embarrassment in it; they'd known each other too long for that. She lowered her guard as the comfort of the familiar wrapped itself around her. Troubling questions faded in the subsequent flood of sensations: the numbness of her bruised and swollen face, her nipples tightening in anticipation of the hot water, the stiff cleanliness of the wool carpet beneath her feet. As she walked across it, she watched Sophie stir the water with a wooden spoon. She somehow managed to make even this event erotic. Smiling, Sophie gestured her toward the basin with a nod.

Corbeau stepped into the water, her toes splaying with the pleasure of it: hot and clean and untouched by another person. She moaned softly as Sophie began to dab at her lacerations. As Sophie moved the wet, steaming cloth over her skin, Corbeau luxuriated in the simple pleasure of touch. How long had it been since she had been touched like this—gently, kindly, without agenda? She had told herself so often that she didn't need it, she had almost come to believe it. The wet cloth wiping her shoulders clean, tracing her breasts and hip gave the lie to it all. Corbeau whimpered as the cloth pressed insistently at a yellowing bruise, as if to wipe it away. Even if there was no future together outside of those rooms, even if in a few hours Corbeau would slip away again into the night, for the moment she wasn't so absolutely alone. Could she ever be again? It was the same every time she found herself on Rue St. Dominique. That was the reason, she remembered—much too late now—that each time she swore it would be the last.

It still required a conscious effort to let someone take care of her. But at that moment, it was an effort she was willing to make.

She sighed as Sophie anointed her head with steaming, clear water again and again, working it through her hair with practiced fingers. Expert fingertips loosened the muscles of her shoulders and back, and her burdens fell away until she feared that, without them, she might float up through the ceiling and away into the clouds.

Then another rush of water.

A stiff brush on her back.

"You said Madame Boucher's group was meeting tonight," Corbeau said, surfacing from her ruminations.

"Shh. Close your eyes."

The water rose in the basin and grew hotter. A bowl brushed her ankle and poured hot, rose-scented water over her head once, twice, until her hair ran smooth and clean down her back.

"God, that's good."

Sophie remained silent, but Corbeau could feel satisfaction radiating from her as she lifted Corbeau's arm and ran a moist cloth over the dark hair beneath it. Sophie had told her once about resorts where the wealthy could bathe as often as they liked in natural hot springs. Some or other paramour had promised to take her there once, but his infatuation had ended before he could make good on it. Corbeau didn't share the Church's belief in the sinfulness of bathing. It did seem as if it would be a good conduit for disease if too many people were involved. But she and Sophie were only two, and how could anything this good be wrong?

Another bowl of water cascaded down her back. A warm, clean cloth followed, over her shoulder, under her arm, over her flat buttocks. She sucked in her breath as another hand cupped one of her small breasts, thumb teasing the stiff brown nipple.

"There's no sin in a mutual exchange of pleasure," Sophie purred. Corbeau reached for her, but, giggling softly, Sophie moved out of reach. Her hands continued their exploration of Corbeau's lean, muscular limbs, fingers deftly applying healing unguents to old scars and new bruises, flirting with the edges of her most intimate crevices.

"I don't care if there is," Corbeau breathed.

Sophie's attentions suddenly stopped. "You should care, Elise. You should care as if your soul depends on it."

Corbeau blinked. As her eyes adjusted to being open again, the soft light of the paraffin lamps seemed suddenly harsh. "I don't understand you, sometimes," Corbeau said.

Sophie's careful mask slipped, and Corbeau caught a glimpse of something cunning before it retreated and Sophie's pleasant expression returned.

"Enough talk. Come to bed, now."

As Corbeau stepped out of the basin, Sophie wrapped a clean sheet around her shoulders. A mixture of scents rose with the steam: rose oil, eucalyptus from one of the ointments, and a combination of flowers and olive oil from the expensive Italian soaps. The moment wasn't completely broken, but Corbeau was back on her guard. The heat from the fire raised goose bumps on her legs. But despite her suspicion, if she was going to get anything useful out of this encounter, she'd have to avoid her natural inclination to push.

She pulled Sophie close, as if to reiterate her commitment to their silent agreement to suspend hostilities. Sophie melted into her arms, and their mouths found each other, their bodies fitting together as if they'd never been apart.

"But you will, at some point, tell me—" Corbeau said.

Instead of the flash of anger Corbeau expected, Sophie smiled and pressed a fingertip to her lips. "Yes, Elise. All that and more."

The first thing Corbeau had noticed about Sophie was her skin.

She was then, as now, fastidiously, eccentrically clean. A libertine, a hedonist, from the glass of wine in her upraised hand to the pointed tips of her newly polished boots. Even before Corbeau had shut the wine-bar door behind herself that night so long ago, she had known that the young woman at the bar, who had stared at her as if there were nothing and no one else in the world, would be as soft as velvet and would smell and taste of soap.

Corbeau remembered how pale her skin had looked even in the windowless, candlelit dim, the air thick with smoke, spilled wine, and perfumes. They were both nineteen, and Sophie had been laughing at something someone had said. Until her eyes and Corbeau's had locked.

"Stop thinking," Sophie whispered. She took Corbeau's chin in her hand and turned it away from the window, drawn curtains transforming early afternoon to night. They were standing in the doorway of the bedroom, Corbeau still half-wrapped in the sheet, and Sophie finally shedding her layers of clothes.

"Would you believe me if I said I was thinking about you?"

Lips to skin, the soft skin right behind Sophie's ear. She still tasted of soap, only now it was the expensive, flower-scented kind—the kind one gives as a gift to a lover—rather than the everyday, coarse blend of animal fat and lye. Who was giving her soap like that? Corbeau wondered.

Not that it was any of her business.

"I'm right here," Sophie said.

"I'm sorry."

A shoulder, sinewy and hard; a reminder of the rough streets from whence they both had come. A small, perfectly formed breast, pink nipple rising to the familiar brush of Corbeau's fingertips— never familiar enough to foster contempt—not this time. It had been a mistake to expect a flower to grow in a dank basement rank with the fumes of distillation and furious work—a mistake Corbeau would not make again. When Sophie had left all those years ago, in a storm of frustration and broken glass, Corbeau had secretly thought her departure well deserved.

"Would you rather just—oh."

She was already wet, and Corbeau slid inside easily. Corbeau laid her back, across the mattress, across the heavy feather bed, and lay down beside her, left leg over left leg, circling her thumb around the spot that always made Sophie sigh. Sophie began to say something else, but Corbeau sealed her mouth with a kiss. For a while she let Sophie ride her fingers, moving slowly in the tight, familiar heat, until she felt Sophie's hips rise and heard her breath catch.

"Not yet," Corbeau whispered.

"Elise!"

Ignoring her protests, Corbeau withdrew her hand and pulled Sophie's leg tighter between her own. She brought her fingers to her lips. "Civet and rose. A woman's choice."

"Beast. Are you jealous?"

"Maybe."

Sophie seemed pleased by the idea and wriggled closer. Corbeau's sex pulsed in response. Right there, right then, she could have forgotten that it always started this way: the ever-present spark of desire fanned into a small but manageable fire, the heat between them comfortable but passionate. Right there and then she might even have forgotten the reason she'd come back to Rue St. Dominique in the first place, or the inevitable explosion that would follow when they'd again reached their age-old impasse.

Corbeau cleared her throat. Her fingers combed Sophie's hair into a flame-colored fan. "You said Madame Boucher's group was meeting tonight. Care to elaborate?"

For a moment Sophie looked as if she were going to bite, but she sighed and pulled herself back up against a stack of pillows. She ran a hand over her face, irritated but resigned. "At her house on the right bank. It's a horrible place. One of those new houses the bourgeoisie put up to pretend they're noble."

"But Madame Boucher is noble," Corbeau said.

Rolling her eyes, Sophie turned onto her side and propped herself up on an elbow.

"Some ancestor managed to buy a title a ways back, it's true. They even had a family emblem drawn up at some point. But they were, and remain, penniless. Her late husband, Henri, was the one with the money. Common as they come, though. The oldest story in the world. Anyway, the house is a monstrosity, surrounded by other monstrosities, all dressed up to look like something less monstrous. She even had them carve that emblem in stone and place it above the door."

Corbeau smiled and ran a hand over the gentle swell of Sophie's hip, lazily tracing around the navel with her thumb. This new contempt was a far cry from her earlier worshipful description of Madame Boucher. Was she compensating for having deliberately made Corbeau jealous?

"And they're meeting when?" Corbeau asked, slipping her hand between Sophie's tightly closed thighs.

"No civilized dinner begins before nine."

"It's a dinner?"

"A party, even, if you can imagine."

"With their leader missing?"

Sophie sat up abruptly, pulling herself and her pillow against the headboard.

"She'll be fine, I told you. You need to have faith."

"Sounds like you've got faith enough for both of us. And I don't know what to make of that, Soph."

"People change."

"I suppose."

The heat between them began to drain away, and for the first time, Corbeau felt how cold the room was despite the fireplace just beyond the doorway. She pulled the covers back, and they both slid underneath.

"Will they be choosing an interim leader?" Corbeau said.

"I don't know. I certainly wasn't invited."

"Did you expect to be?"

The silence said more than words. If Corbeau was reading things correctly, she had been right about how close Sophie and Madame Boucher had been. If Corbeau was reading things correctly, the civet and rose soaps had been Hermine Boucher's choice. How long had they been together? If Sophie was being excluded from that night's meeting, then she probably hadn't been more than a peripheral member of the Church of the Divine Spark.

But she knew the Church's work and its goals. And she'd been on intimate terms with its leader. Still, something had changed between them before Madame Boucher disappeared.

Something making Sophie deeply unhappy.

"When was the last time *you* saw Hermine Boucher?" Corbeau asked gently.

Sophie looked away this time. Outside the rain was falling again: as hard against the evenly paved streets in front of Sophie's building as it was no doubt onto the cracking roof-tiles of Corbeau's. Sophie shivered, and Corbeau pulled the feather bed farther over them.

Sophie laid her head on Corbeau's shoulder. "The demons were at her again the night before she disappeared. I brewed her up something quick, like I'd done a thousand times, but it wasn't working anymore. She was this close to begging that Gypsy woman to come back. Said she was ready to try to handle it a different way." Sophie looked up from Corbeau's shoulder, bitterness plain on her face.

"Did she call her back?" Corbeau asked.

"No. I stayed with her until it was time to go to the party—another party to which I wasn't invited. Neither was Dr. Kalderash, though she turned up that night all the same. And then…"

It was a strange position in which to find oneself, lying naked next to someone, sympathizing that her lover wanted someone else. But they had no claim on each other, and they'd known each other too long for either of them to be either upset or surprised.

The unwelcome thought occurred to Corbeau that Sophie had just revealed a possible motive for disposing of Madame Boucher herself, or at least for seeing Dr. Kalderash take the blame for it. She glanced over at the other woman, who was running a finger over the embroidery on the featherbed. Sophie was angry and jealous, yes. Corbeau had seen for herself that she was capable of violence. At the same time, she seemed so convinced Hermine Boucher would surface at some point, safe and unharmed. It wasn't the viewpoint one would expect from a kidnapper. Sophie's fingers strayed over the edge of the feather bed and, with a glance to the left, burrowed under the covers as if in search of warmth.

"You'll go tonight," Sophie whispered, as her fingers found their target. Corbeau's hips moved forward to meet them, and as Sophie leaned forward to steal a kiss, Corbeau pressed herself closer.

"I'll go."

"The housekeeper's name is Madame Pettit," Sophie whispered. "Take what you want from my clothes, but I assume you'll be entering through the back."

Corbeau smiled against Sophie's lips. Sophie had heard enough of her stories to anticipate how Corbeau would go about gaining entrance to the house. She moved her hand over Sophie's firm, round buttock.

"I always have enjoyed the back entrance," she murmured.

Business concluded, she followed Sophie into the warmth beneath the feather bed. She had other questions, of course, but Corbeau had gotten the information she needed, and quite a bit more. Familiar fingers described tingling trails across her legs, stomach, and breasts. She moaned softly as something she'd thought forgotten stirred deep within her. Encouraged, Sophie slid down the length of her body, pressing her legs open and insinuating herself between them. And then all was as it had been in the beginning: everything and nothing, just pounding pulse and darkness, scent, and skin.

❖

Night came quickly, and with it, the chiming of the mantel clock and a renewed deluge outside the now-darkened window. The sun had receded, dragging night's black cloak over Paris while Sophie slept on beside her. Corbeau's body felt heavy and sated, but she had awakened with her mind afire with questions. Thunder shook the wooden frame of the building. Still deep in the clutches of some dream—a pleasant one, from her expression—

Sophie mewled in her sleep and turned over. The faint smells of sweat and rose oil hung in the air. It would be so easy to burrow back beneath the covers and luxuriate in Sophie's warm, clean flesh. If she left now, Sophie would make her pay. On the other hand, Sophie had been the one who had told her about the meeting. She shouldn't be surprised if Corbeau actually went.

Bunching her pillow against the headboard, she sat up and gave the cool night air a moment to clear her mind. Then she slid from under the covers and stood.

Shivering in the evening chill, Corbeau fumbled across the room to the wardrobe for a linen shift. Sophie had told her to take what she wanted, and in the dim light of the outside streetlamps, she considered three different dresses. But Sophie had guessed right, that Corbeau would try to lose herself in the downstairs bustle rather than walk in through the front door. If the Church of the Divine Spark was throwing a party at Madame Boucher's house, they would probably have hired outside help for the evening. And none of Sophie's dresses, designed, made, and bought under the watchful supervision of her wealthy benefactors, would be appropriate to the task. But she would help herself to a clean shift, she thought, selecting the best one. She stole a glance at herself in the mirror near the vanity. The garment was too short and too big in the bust and hips, but the linen felt divine against her skin. It would do. She padded back out to the main room to gather her things.

At some point while Corbeau had slept, Sophie had carefully laid out her dress and stockings to dry. She had put away the basin and accoutrements, hung the kettle back up on its hook, and returned the soaps and oils to their places. The fire had died to coals, but the room was warm. Corbeau didn't look forward to being back outside pounding the wet pavement without Javert's umbrella. On the other hand, part of her had been itching to leave since she'd awakened. These little trysts were fun, but every time she left, the empty ache inside grew darker and deeper. They were using each other—no one was being deceived. Yet Corbeau couldn't deny they both wanted—they both deserved—more than this. Sophie wouldn't be satisfied to go back to near-poverty, nor to the poverty of attention that was the lot of police wives. As for Corbeau, she could hardly take care of herself. She needed a partner who could entertain herself—someone who would be happy to look after her own needs, and maybe some of Corbeau's needs as well.

Her shoulder bag lay atop the dress. Corbeau drew a sharp breath when she saw Javert's papers had been gone through then straightened again, a little too much, as if to compensate for the trespass. She checked her bottles and prayer book. The bottles—both the ones she had brought from her apartment and the one she'd found under Lambert's bed—were intact and accounted for. The prayer book, not surprisingly, was untouched. Irritation flared in her chest. Sophie had always been one for prying—subtly, by manipulating the conversation, as well as through plain snooping. It was what enabled her to collect the most valuable information for the newspapers. But on a personal level, it was irritating as hell. Considering the degree to which Sophie had mixed herself up in the case, it was dangerous as well.

Cursing under her breath, Corbeau tugged on her now-stiff stockings and pulled the scratchy wool dress back over her head. She checked the contents of her bag again and swung it back over her shoulder. She shuffled into her boots and coat.

She still couldn't figure out why the Church of the Divine Spark would be throwing a party when their leader was missing. A meeting, she could understand. If the organization had come to the same conclusion that Corbeau had—that Hermine Boucher had met with a bad end—they would have to decide whether, and how, to carry on her work. Leadership would be reconfigured. But a dinner party—that was bizarre.

But what if the party was concealing a meeting? If there had been a conspiracy to get rid of Hermine Boucher, perhaps it wasn't a case of disgruntled servants. What if certain members of the Divine Spark had decided to take the organization in a different direction? The Church had made a name for itself doing good works, but it had also begun to involve itself in what Sophie thought of as suppressing demonic activity. What if the differences between these two functions had widened into a schism? Moreover, the Church's deviation from Catholic doctrine had made Madame Boucher an enemy—or at least an irritant—to the King. Could a few enterprising members of the Church of the Divine Spark be aiming to give the movement a political edge?

Could a power struggle within the organization have resulted in Madame Boucher's disappearance?

Corbeau glanced at the bedroom door, behind which Sophie slept on. It was tempting to wake her and ask her opinion, as someone so close to the situation. On the other hand, Sophie was close enough to the situation that any answers she did offer would have to be weighed and examined accordingly. Corbeau didn't have the time.

No. She would go to the party as planned, though she wouldn't ask for Madame Pettit, as Sophie instructed. It would be good to have a name to drop if she found herself in a pinch, but she would find her own way inside and draw her own conclusions.

Corbeau gave the room one last glance before buttoning up her coat. The coals smoldered gently behind the dragonfly screen. Her eyes traveled over the familiar shapes of the furniture, the neatly folded canvas, where she'd had what would likely be her last bath for a long time, across the statues on the mantel.

And then she saw something she was certain hadn't been there before. It was a small, stopper-topped phial, similar to the one she had found in Armand Lambert's room. The liquid inside it glittered in the lamplight.

Corbeau crossed the room quickly. She snatched the bottle from the mantel and popped off the cork. She could identify several ingredients by smell, but she'd no idea what they could mean in combination. A chill shivered through her.

"What are you playing at?" she asked, glancing at the door, behind which Sophie slumbered.

Sophie had placed the phial there. Placed it there for Corbeau to find, along with her dried clothes and obviously examined documents. Was Sophie telling her that she, too, had figured out the connection among Lambert, Bertrand, and Fournier? Or perhaps she was telling her Paris had a new alchemist. The Montagne Ste. Geneviève victims had to have gotten their little phials from someone—someone lacking either skill or patience, from the side effects Corbeau had witnessed. Or it could have been a coincidence. But true coincidences were rare. The fact that Corbeau had protected Sophie while she and Vidocq had dismantled Corbeau's criminal network damned both of them. But what exactly was Sophie's role in this? And what was the purpose of revealing the depths of her involvement to Corbeau?

Corbeau slipped the new phial into her shoulder bag. The formulae inside the two phials would give her a better clue about what was going on. She would analyze them at home. But first she had to find Javert. And before that, she had to pay a visit to the home of the missing Hermine Boucher.

In the back room, Sophie stirred again. Guilt, responsibility, suspicion, and affection wrestled uncomfortably in Corbeau's chest. It was always so good in Sophie's soft, wide bed. So easy to forget all her troubles. But the moment she pulled the covers back, the emptiness wrapped around her like a suffocating cloak, and she knew she had to leave, for both their sakes. Outside, rain was falling—curtains of cold, black drops as large and as hard as bullets. And her with no umbrella.

Silently, so as not to wake Sophie, Corbeau crept back across the main room and through the bedroom door. She lingered a moment, almost hoping that Sophie would wake at her touch. She bent down and kissed her forehead.

She turned abruptly and left before it was too late.

## CHAPTER NINE

Hermine Boucher's house rose from the street in a bold display of light stone, ironwork, and rounded arches. Three stories high but not very wide, it stood apart from its neighbors and was separated from the street by a curving paved driveway fronted by an iron gate. It was an attractive, well-built home, recently erected, though Corbeau could see how both the design and the newness would strike Sophie's sensibilities the wrong way. Some of Paris's most prominent citizens lived on the surrounding streets. However, the nearby houses seemed to bask in the rude ostentation of new wealth.

The rain had slowed to a heavy drip, and Corbeau caught sight of the carved stone above the front door, just like Sophie had said. Disappointingly, the darkness obscured the details of the design. But Corbeau had seen plenty of emblems like it. Modeled on the coats of arms that had fallen out of fashion before Corbeau was born, the design doubtless featured a distorted shield, a weapon, and some fierce-looking animal. Many would have considered such a thing gauche, but for Madame Boucher, her family's marginal nobility—bought by an ancestor's bribe and maintained over generations through careful idleness and avoidance of taxes—would have been her primary contribution to her marriage. Her late husband had likely seized with both hands the opportunity to bring whatever prestige he could to his new money.

The windows glowed warmly, two on each side of the front door, revealing the silhouettes of elegantly dressed guests. Corbeau wondered how many of them had given a thought to the mistress of the house, currently being held against her will somewhere out in the cold, dark night. Were they carrying on because they thought the widow Boucher would have wanted it that way? Did they have faith, as Sophie did? Or did the swirling shadows and strains of sedate music hide a darker intention?

Corbeau removed the Bureau insignia from her collar and pinned it to the inside of her coat pocket. She'd learned her lesson in Dr. Kalderash's doorway. This was a household steeped in the occult. No doubt someone she encountered would have had traffic with the Bureau before it had been disbanded. She kept walking past the gate until she found the gap where the hedge that bordered the neighboring property met the stone pillar that held the gate in place. Just as Corbeau had expected, the gate was more for show than security. She slipped through the gap. Keeping in the shadows of the hedge, she made her way around the side of the house.

Muddled snatches of conversation sounded faintly through the thick glass. Corbeau shrank back into the shadows. She didn't expect to encounter anyone outside at this time and in this weather but kept Madame Pettit's name on her lips just the same. She followed the driveway around the side of the house, then dashed across wet grass to the back entrance. The driveway led to a single-carriage carriage house on the back corner of the property. It occurred to her that behind its wooden doors, the structure might conceal the very carriage from which Madame Boucher had disappeared. She would have a look, after getting the information she needed from inside the house.

Crouching in the shelter of the back stairs, she made quick work of the back-door lock and let herself inside. The stairs continued down a dark passage toward the kitchen. Voices echoed up from the depths of the servant areas below the stairs, accompanied by the aromas of roasting meats and fresh bread.

Corbeau's stomach growled. It had been a long time since her breakfast at Oubliette. She wished she trusted Sophie enough to go look for the housekeeper directly. She might well have been given a bite to eat at that point.

Off to the right, a narrower staircase led up to the main house. Floorboards creaked above her head, and the walls hummed with conversation and laughter. If only she had an easy way of mingling with the guests—what information she might have gleaned there! On the other hand, servants were the unseen eyes and ears of every house, and often prone to gossip. If she could pass herself off as help hired for the evening, she could learn what she might from the staff, then possibly find an excuse to poke about upstairs.

"Who are you? How did you get in here? Where do you think you're going?"

Corbeau flinched at the voice suddenly at her shoulder and was just quick enough to stop herself from dislocating the hand that closed over her elbow. It was a woman's hand, work-hardened but with thin bones. No threat there.

Corbeau turned slowly, deliberately, calling up her story. "I'm looking for Madame Pettit, the housekeeper. I've come to work."

"You found her." Madame Pettit was fiftyish, all angles and points, with a dark uniform and salt-and-pepper hair pulled up severely. She looked Corbeau up and down. "You're Moreau the Alchemist?"

*What?* Corbeau's heart raced.

The woman continued without waiting for an answer. "Mademoiselle Martin told us to expect you tonight. She didn't say you were a woman, however. And she didn't say you'd look like you'd been in a fight."

Corbeau's heart stopped altogether.

*Sophie had set her up.*

As Corbeau had suspected, the phial on Sophie's mantel had indeed been a message. The Church of the Divine Spark had acquired an alchemist—only everyone seemed to know it except the alchemist herself. She remembered the reverent way in which Sophie had described Madame Boucher and her organization earlier that morning in Oubliette. She'd been testing the waters, testing Corbeau's potential interest. When she realized Corbeau was only interested in the organization as it related to the investigation, Sophie had used this as bait.

And now Corbeau was exactly where Sophie had wanted her.

But she was also in a unique, and arguably better, position.

Corbeau mumbled an apology for her appearance. She had forgotten the bruises and lacerations. Her coat was dripping brown water onto the floorboards, and the dress underneath it, quite frankly, would need to be burned.

"I've seen worse," the housekeeper responded after a moment. "And though I can't countenance wasting money on perfume and baths, it at least makes up for that dress. Now follow me. Your lab is set up, and you've a lot of work to do."

Corbeau's heart sank as the housekeeper took her own coat from a row of hooks near the door, but she followed her back outside. As they sloshed through the mire of wet grass toward the carriage house, her hopes rose again. She might have to work harder to find an excuse to get back in the house, but Madame Pettit was giving her an engraved invitation to a building she would have had to break into. The housekeeper led her around the back of the structure and took a ring of keys from her belt. "In here. It's not much, but it's out of the rain, and you won't disturb anyone."

They stepped into a four-horse stable, walked past a matched pair of bays, and stopped at the last stall: a large double box, secured with a padlock. Corbeau glanced at the back wall, where a sliding double door in the center connected the stable with the carriage area. Madame Pettit unlocked the stall and gestured Corbeau inside.

Tables sat against three of the walls. The tables were neatly arrayed with tubes, pipettes, flasks, phials, and clamps. There were two burners and a hot plate, all with new wicks and full of oil. Shelves lined the walls above the tables with an impressive assortment of bottles stopped with corks or sealed with wax. An apron hung on the back of the door. A man's shirt and trousers, clean and folded, had been placed on the corner of one of the tables for her to change in to while she worked. There was also a cap, which would serve to keep noxious and flammable fumes from her hair. Corbeau's pulse quickened. It felt good to be back in a laboratory again. While Madame Pettit spoke, Corbeau began to mentally assemble the tubes and clamps into a still and to organize the bottles according to their properties.

"Mademoiselle Martin told us more or less what kind of equipment you'd need, but none of us was sure how to set it up. She said you'd know how."

"Thank you."

The larger vessels contained the alcohol and oils essential for distillation. She also noted a number of more esoteric ingredients—plants and tinctures not easily accessible to the everyday tinkerer. The layout resembled the basement lab Corbeau had once maintained. Sophie had remembered well.

Madame Pettit cleared her throat. "I assume you've already been briefed on your task. Is there anything else you need before you get started?"

Corbeau tore her thoughts from the equipment and forced her gaze back to the housekeeper. "Only to express my condolences on the recent loss of your mistress. Such a charismatic leader. It's amazing that everyone seems to go on so well, even in her absence. I do hope it won't take long for her to be found, safe and sound."

Madame Pettit pierced her with a long, unwavering look. If she felt anything about the situation, she hid it well. "That's none of your concern. Now get started. I don't need to tell you that time is of the essence." Corbeau watched her walk away. When she reached the door, Madame Pettit turned. "I'll have someone bring you something to eat in a little while. You'll find an apron on the wall and clothing to wear while you're here. The Great Prophet was very clear that no traces of your work should leave with you." And with that, she shut the door.

*The Great Prophet?* Wasn't that how Sophie had referred to Madame Boucher? How quickly the group had found a new leader! Had Sophie been aware of the change before she sent Corbeau to the house? Her heart thrummed. It felt like she had less information than when she'd left the Rue St. Dominique, and less reason to trust the information that remained. She had to think. Quickly, automatically, her hands found the familiar clamps and pipettes. As her mind raced, she began to build a still from memory.

The Divine Spark must have intended for her to create a formula for subduing untrained supernatural talents on a mass scale. Sophie hadn't mentioned any such thing, but it wasn't difficult to figure out.

Sophie had put her at the center of the operation, and possibly mere steps from the carriage from which Madame Boucher had disappeared. Corbeau couldn't have engineered a better situation. Yet the thought that Sophie had manipulated her into it set her on edge. Sophie had known she wouldn't have willingly gone back to the business that had sent her to prison, yet she'd wanted Corbeau to join the organization so badly she'd put her in that exact position. Sophie had probably hoped that once Corbeau arrived, she would forget the suffering she'd caused all those years ago and fall back in love with the work itself. Perhaps even be grateful. Perhaps Sophie had thought, if Madame Boucher didn't want her, then she and Corbeau could return to some semblance of what they'd had before Corbeau's arrest and transformation.

But was Sophie working for Madame Boucher or for the new Prophet?

Either way, what a feather in Sophie's cap, to have produced Moreau the Alchemist, back from the dead, or prison, or from wherever people had thought she'd disappeared—especially considering the sloppy work their current alchemist was turning out. The more Corbeau thought about it, the more she wondered if the outbursts in the Montagne Ste. Geneviève weren't due simply to impurities in the formulae the victims had been using—or even to solutions badly formulated in the first place. A cold dread settled in her bowels. Sophie had mentioned she'd tried her hand at putting together the occasional brew to help Madame Boucher suppress her overactive spiritual forces. It wasn't difficult to do—much of the time a mild sedative would do the trick. But Sophie hadn't been up to anything more complex than that, and she'd known it. Corbeau shuddered at the thought of Sophie trying to reconstruct the work they'd done together all those years ago.

Corbeau shucked off her coat and dress and gratefully slipped into the clean, albeit well-worn trousers and shirt. If the stable had contained a heat source larger than a brazier, she would have happily tossed the ruined dress onto it. Soiled as it was with her blood and sweat, it surely wouldn't be wise to leave it lying around in a place crawling with occult practitioners. She wadded it up and kicked it under the table. The shirt and trousers fit well. Vidocq had insisted his female agents wear trousers when not working undercover, for the freedom of movement they afforded. It hadn't taken Corbeau long to get used to it. The new chief inspector hadn't been able to fire her, but he did force her back into a dress—a fact that Corbeau resented almost as bitterly as all the man's other insults combined.

Comfortable once more, she examined her supplies. Paper and pencils for taking down notes. Boxes of plant matter: flowers, grasses, roots, and herbs. Oil and alcohol in abundance. A good supply of empty bottles with corks for holding the mixtures she was to create. And the still she'd assembled, so quickly and almost without thinking about it. Sophie had done a good job.

Corbeau shook her head. Whatever was happening with the Church of the Divine Spark, Sophie was in it to her neck. How had she known Lambert would have an attack? And how had she known to find Corbeau there? The Montagne Ste. Geneviève was not at all close to Rue St. Dominique. Nothing else of interest to a gossipmonger happened there. Had Bertrand and Fournier been tests to see whether Corbeau would respond? Had they been lures? Corbeau pushed away her darker thoughts. It was time to see what was in those bottles.

Her fingers shook as she removed the two phials from her shoulder bag. The names and faces of the people she'd harmed so long ago rose up in her mind's eye, accusing. She heard Joseph's cry as he fell under the carriage wheels just out of her reach. The list of names Vidocq had read to her that first night beneath the Conciergerie—names of people she'd sent to the madhouse, to prison, to their graves—scrolled through her mind, permanently etched there. Corbeau hadn't allowed herself a laboratory after that, outside of the Bureau's compounding room. As much as standing before a burner again excited her, it terrified her twice over.

Pushing the dark thoughts aside, she popped the cork on Lambert's bottle. She sniffed it and wrote down the ingredients she could smell. She put a bit on her tongue to divine a few more. It was basically a sedative, not much different from the ones in her mother's pillbox. An inelegant concoction, but one that would take the edge off an outburst. Something a student might have made. Or an apprentice who had watched over the shoulder of a master for many years, then tried to duplicate what he had seen.

What *she* had seen.

"What have you done, girl?" she asked, as if Sophie could have heard and answered. Her dread increasing, she took the bottle she'd found on Sophie's mantel and performed the same tests. The liquid inside was likewise colorless, but the smell was distinctly different. The taste was astringent. Grassy. Perhaps a bit of wormwood, but she couldn't be certain. Corbeau lit the wick of the oil burner and wiped clean the metal plate that rested on a stand above it. After it had heated, she used a pipette to drop a small amount of the solution onto the plate. Seconds later, the liquid burnt down to nothing, leaving no telltale residues, save for a sweet-smelling smoke that disappeared almost as quickly as it had formed. "Damn it, Sophie, what the hell was it?"

If only she had more time. But at least the tests had confirmed what Madame Boucher's group was up to. And she was fairly certain why Lambert, Bertrand, and Fournier had suffered their outbursts. She didn't know what had become of Madame Boucher, though she was certain that whatever it was, Dr. Kalderash had something to do with it. Whether or not Lambert, Bertrand, and Fournier had been Kalderash's co-conspirators—that remained to be seen. And if Madame Boucher's carriage lay behind those double doors, Corbeau suspected she would find answers to at least some of these questions inside.

She pinched out the flame under the burner, replaced the stoppers in the bottles, and placed the bottles carefully back into her bag. She glanced at the dress by her feet, then picked it up and draped it over her shoulder, turned off the lamp, and exited the makeshift lab, locking the door behind her. There was another lock on the double doors between the stable and the carriage room, but the tumblers gave way easily beneath her picks. She pushed the doors aside.

In the muted light the moon cast through clouds and window, she recognized Madame Boucher's carriage. The well-kept two-seater sat in the middle of the carriage room, its new black paint gleaming dully. Taking a lantern from its hook, Corbeau pulled the doors shut behind her. Slowly, she began to circle the carriage. The vehicle was new. The wheels showed little wear, and the paint—it hadn't been painted more than once—was intact. As she passed around the back and around the other side, she stopped. The frame of the window wasn't sitting quite flush with the body of the vehicle. Holding up the lantern, she peered inside.

The interior of the carriage looked as pristine as the outside. The bench on the far side was well and expensively padded in shiny black leather, though her position was inadequate for examining the rest of the vehicle. She circled around to the doors, running her fingers over the smooth metal handle before opening the door. As she did, something flew out, bounced off the step, and disappeared into the loose dirt near her boot. Corbeau knelt down and retrieved a brass button. Angling it into the lamplight, she smiled. She'd been right about Madame Boucher's family emblem: a distorted shield—wider than it was tall—with a bear rampant on either side and crossed swords at the center. Designed to recall the feudal nobility diluted by time and social change, the emblem probably didn't date back more than fifty years.

But that wasn't important.

The button had come from a man's garment—likely from livery. But who would have lost a button inside the carriage? Drivers and footmen wore livery but had no business inside a carriage. Those who did, like Claudine Fournier, would not wear livery. Perhaps Madame Boucher had been having an affair with Lambert or Bertrand. Perhaps the button had come off during some late-night assignation.

She set the lantern on the floor of the carriage and sat down beside it. From that position, the window frame looked even more warped than it had from the outside. Her gaze traveled over the new upholstery, across the overstuffed seat, and stopped. The seat cushion opposite the window looked normal, but the one beneath the window looked lumpy and odd. In a new carriage such as this, where the leather upholstery was still stiff, the stuffing should have been evenly distributed. But it wasn't. One side was visibly higher than the other.

Tucking the button into her trouser pocket, Corbeau slid onto the floor of the carriage and felt around the underside of the seat where it hung over the base. A few of the tacks that held the leather to the seat stuck out unevenly. They rocked in their holes under gentle pressure from her fingers. Someone had removed them, Corbeau realized, and replaced them none too carefully. Closer inspection revealed visible holes in the leather where the tacks held the leather to the wood. The leather had stretched to accommodate the greater bulk of whatever was beneath the leather. Someone had indeed removed the tacks.

Corbeau worked the tacks out one by one and placed them on the floor beside her. Then she plunged her hand under the leather.

"Good God."

She had reached inside, expecting the horsehair that generally filled carriage cushions. But her fingers met silk instead. Carefully, she enticed the gown out from beneath the leather. She shook it out and held it up, squinting at it in the dim light of the lantern.

"I'll be damned."

Glinting crystal beads formed an intricate design over champagne-colored silk. It was the same dress Hermine Boucher had been wearing in the newspaper sketch that appeared the day after she vanished. Corbeau glanced again at the window, whose frame sat so unevenly in its place. She felt the livery button pressing against her thigh. Immediately, she knew exactly what had happened.

Hermine Boucher's preference for simple, straight gowns uncomplicated by whalebone hoops, extra petticoats, or bustles— dresses her mother might have worn in her youth—had been a boon to newspaper satirists. Her dislike of skirts a carriage could hide beneath had been described as old-fashioned, eccentric, and unfortunate.

But had Hermine Boucher subscribed to the fashions of the day, she never would have been able to make herself disappear in such a spectacular manner.

The scene came together in Corbeau's mind, as clearly as if she were watching it happen. Hermine Boucher had entered the carriage in her gown, accompanied by her companion, Claudine Fournier. Michel Bertrand had been driving. Footman Lambert had helped the ladies inside, and then he had run along beside the carriage once it started, as was the fashion. Inside, Mademoiselle Fournier had helped Madame out of her gown and into the livery they had placed there earlier. At some point, the carriage passed under a bridge or through a sparsely populated area. Dressed in livery, Madame had exited the carriage through the window— witnesses at the party had reported the footman had locked the door behind her as she entered. Anyone watching when the carriage emerged would have seen Hermine Boucher—by all accounts a tall woman with a mannish, athletic build—in livery, and assumed it was the footman. Lambert left the carriage long enough for Madame Boucher to duck into the shadows, then rejoined it before it reached the house.

Which proved Lambert and Fournier, and probably Michel Bertrand as well, had been accomplices.

And Maria Kalderash was innocent. There had been no kidnapping at all.

Prefect Javert was trying to frame Dr. Kalderash for a crime that never happened. For surely if he had been serious about investigating Madame's supposed disappearance, he and his men would have gone over the carriage in great detail and come to the same conclusions she had.

But why would Madame Boucher want to disappear? And why did everyone else want Dr. Kalderash to hang for it?

It was clear why Sophie would benefit from having Dr. Kalderash out of the picture. Kalderash had been a rival for Madame Boucher's affections, and even if Madame didn't return to Sophie's embrace, Sophie was just vindictive enough to rejoice in her rival's ruin. Obviously, Sophie had known about the entire operation. As much as her heart was breaking over Hermine Boucher's rejection, she hadn't seemed a bit worried about her disappearance. She had known, and she hadn't said anything. In fact, like Javert, she had gone out of her way to implicate Dr. Kalderash.

But what was Javert's excuse?

Damn it.

Was Madame Boucher hoping her disappearance would draw more attention to her group's good works? Or was she hoping to escape the wrath of the Church and the King, who were busily prosecuting people who stepped out of line with their moral teachings?

Or was there another explanation?

Corbeau crammed her hated, police-issue dress into the cavity beneath the upholstery. Then, finding a weak spot in the stitching beneath the arm of Madame Boucher's dress, she pulled and worked at the stitching until the arm came apart from the bodice. She folded the arm and stuffed it into her shoulder bag, then shoved Madame Boucher's dress back into the cushion with her own. Finally she replaced the tacks.

She would take the evidence of Dr. Kalderash's innocence to Javert at his home and rub his nose in it until he told her why.

Relief washed over her. Paris had not treated Dr. Kalderash well. Between Javert's single-minded pursuit of her, the troubles with Madame Boucher, and the fact that Kalderash's nationality would make her a natural target for anyone looking for someone to kick, Corbeau couldn't understand why she hadn't pulled up stakes already. Part of her couldn't help but admire the woman's determination, as brave, or arguably stupid, as it was. And she was relieved that she herself wouldn't add unjust persecution to the woman's troubles.

She sat back against the carriage bench. Rain pounded the roof, but the horses in the next room were peaceful. She found the clean smells of hay and leather calming.

Imagine the strength of character Kalderash must have possessed, for her to press on when everyone who mattered was against her. Imagine what it would be like to have someone like that in one's corner—someone who could stand on her own and had strength to share. Corbeau had never had someone like that in her life. She imagined Madame Boucher had found her presence to be quite a comfort at times, especially when her untrained, unwanted talents flared, and she no doubt felt like her world was falling apart.

No wonder Hermine Boucher had preferred Dr. Kalderash—who had rejected her, soundly—to someone like Sophie, who depended upon her utterly. No wonder Hermine Boucher had pursued Dr. Kalderash to such a ruinous degree, even after Kalderash had left. Corbeau shook her head. As tiresome as her solitary life sometimes was, perhaps it was just as well.

Taking up the lantern, she slid out of the carriage, feet first, and shut the door gently behind her. She was almost to the door when she heard the voices.

"What's his name?"

"Her name…don't know…"

"*Her* name?"

"Madame Pettit said to take her a tray."

"Well, she's gone now. It's all locked up."

"Look, there's a light inside the carriage room."

Cursing silently, Corbeau extinguished the lantern and pressed herself to the wall beside the sliding doors. She held her breath for what felt like an hour, hoping the men would give up and return to the party. Otherwise, how would she explain what she was doing in there? Another few moments passed before she decided to venture a glance through the crack between the doors.

As she peeked out, someone suddenly pulled the doors aside. A hand grabbed her by the collar and pulled her through.

"You!"

Corbeau recognized Vautrin a split second before he slammed her back against the door. The walls of the stable shook. One of the horses bellowed in panic. She locked her arm around Vautrin's and slammed her palm against his elbow—not hard enough to break it, she noted with disappointment. She ducked his punch, but he pulled it back at the last minute and swept her legs out from under her instead. Corbeau sprang to her feet, fists raised, while the second man—who was indeed bearing a tray of food—looked on, appearing stupefied.

"What the devil are you doing here?" Vautrin demanded.

"I might ask you the same thing." When he made no further move to attack, she lowered her hands and brushed off her trousers.

"You've been relieved of your duties. You're a trespasser here."

"I'm here on the prefect's business. What's your excuse?" Corbeau wouldn't have been surprised to learn he was following the Boucher case on his own. As much as he liked to see his own name in the papers, he would have found such a high-profile case irresistible. It certainly would have explained why he had turned up at Lambert's place that night. If so, Vautrin wasn't as stupid as she had assumed. It was a frightening thought. "This is the carriage from which Madame Boucher disappeared," she said.

"Yes, yes, my men have already examined it."

"Really? And what did they find?"

A vein throbbed at Vautrin's temple. He wasn't about to share information with her, his fierce expression said. And if she really were working for Javert, she could go straight to hell. But she could also see curiosity burning behind his dark eyes. Not even Vautrin could have missed the dress inside the seat cushion. He had to have come to the same conclusions she had. Although if that was the case, she'd have expected him to sit back and watch Javert make an idiot of himself, rather than to linger in the carriage house.

Of course he might have come across information she and Javert had overlooked.

"Have you interviewed the staff?" she asked. "Did you get anything sensible out of the footman the other night—Armand Lambert?" She relished the flare of his nostrils when she mentioned Lambert's name. "I trust he's been given the medical attention he needs." Vautrin lunged at her again. She feinted to the side, grabbing a shovel that had been leaning against the wall, and brandished it. "Go on. Give me an excuse."

Corbeau couldn't tell which set him off more, the mention of Lambert or the fact she had questioned him as a colleague might. The chief inspector always had a short fuse, but the murder in his eyes told her that something very wrong had happened to Lambert, and that Vautrin himself was likely responsible.

"Great Prophet?" the other man ventured. More of a boy, Corbeau noticed. Not more than sixteen, and possibly quite a bit less. The tray was shaking in his hands.

"Put it down and leave," Vautrin said quietly. The boy seemed happy to do so.

"You're the Great Prophet?" Corbeau asked as the door slammed shut. "I thought that was Madame Boucher."

"Things change. Drop that damned shovel."

"Not on your life."

Shaking his head, he stepped back. He pushed a clump of hair back over his wide forehead and sighed. "You're the Alchemist, I suppose."

"No, I just came for the hors d'oeuvres."

Vautrin's mouth tightened, but he remained silent. Rain battered the roof as they glared at each other for a long, tense moment.

So this was why Javert had chosen her rather than Vautrin to investigate Madame Boucher's disappearance. If Corbeau hadn't found evidence to the contrary, she could have made the case that Vautrin had done away with Madame Boucher himself, in order to seize control of the Church of the Divine Spark. Oh, how she would have loved to make that case. But by all appearances, Madame Boucher had spirited herself away. And Corbeau couldn't understand why Vautrin, the most pious, sanctimonious zealot she had ever known, would involve himself in a heretical organization in the first place.

But his involvement explained why he had been in the Montagne Ste. Geneviève the other night. He had been tying up loose ends. But was he helping Madame Boucher by getting rid of the people who could disclose that her kidnapping had been a sham? Or was he helping himself by picking off her allies?

One thing was for certain—if Armand Lambert was still alive, he was in great danger. The same went for Claudine Fournier and Michel Bertrand.

But this led back to the question of what Vautrin wanted with the Church of the Divine Spark. Did the group hold some attraction that would make it worth dirtying his hands with heresy? Or perhaps he was trying to co-opt it for a different purpose.

How much did Javert know? His case, as presented, had hinged on Kalderash's motive rather than on physical evidence— evidence that Javert's men would not have missed if they'd undertaken the investigation in any serious way.

Which meant Javert wanted Kalderash for some other reason.

And now that it was clear that Kalderash was innocent, Corbeau was not about to let Javert—or anyone else—get their hands on her without a very good reason.

She was surprised how quickly she was ready to rush to the inventor's defense, considering she'd stormed away from

Kalderash's home swearing to write out an arrest warrant by day's end. But Dr. Kalderash had already suffered so much injustice. A feeling of protectiveness swelled in Corbeau's chest. She would be damned if Maria Kalderash would suffer further on her watch.

"Well, well, well, *Great Prophet*," Corbeau said. The handle of the shovel was slippery with perspiration, and her voice didn't sound as brave as she'd intended. But she pressed him to see if she could provoke him into revelation. "That casts Madame Boucher's disappearance in a rather different light, doesn't it?"

Vautrin's face clouded with rage. Then he seemed to realize the position he was in. Corbeau was investigating at the behest of the prefect of police. And Vautrin had both known Madame Boucher and possessed a good reason for wanting her out of the way.

"It was that Gypsy woman," he sputtered. "Surely even Javert suspects as much."

"Yes, everyone seems to have a reason to want Dr. Kalderash to be guilty. The problem is, there are so many other suspects to choose from."

With the same terrifying quickness he'd exhibited in Lambert's room, Vautrin leaped for the shovel. She swung, but he caught the handle in one hand and deflected the blow with his thick shoulder. He pushed her back toward the wall, and this time, she knew that once he pinned her there, he wouldn't stop. Letting the shovel go, she dropped to the ground and rolled out of the way. Before Vautrin could turn around, she was out the door, disappearing into the cold, black rain.

## CHAPTER TEN

Despite the rain, the Rue des Rosiers wasn't completely deserted, thanks to the newly installed streetlamps shining like beacons through the downpour. Paris had installed gas lighting around the city a little less than ten years ago, and Corbeau wondered how much of the vast reduction in crime in the meantime had been a result of it or, as Vidocq had claimed, to the activities of the Sûreté, which had come into existence at roughly the same time.

From the corner, Corbeau could see that Dr. Kalderash's house was dark. No light shone in the windows, nor was a single lantern hung, despite the legal obligation to do so. Apprehension gathered in her belly as she pushed her way past small groups of people hurrying to get out of the rain. Javert wanted Dr. Kalderash arrested for a crime that hadn't happened. Sophie and Vautrin wanted her out of the way as well—and they had an entire organization of devotees behind them. Hermine Boucher might have wanted Dr. Kalderash back for reasons only the heart could understand, but from what Kalderash had said, the woman was both unstable and violent.

Dr. Kalderash had nowhere to turn. Corbeau had become a police agent in order to right wrongs and to protect the innocent. If anything happened to Maria Kalderash, Corbeau would never forgive herself. She had to tell her what she had found in the carriage house. She had to warn her.

She flung herself onto the doorstep, banging on the door with her fist.

"Doctor!" Thick sheets of rain swallowed her cry, but she struck the door until the windows shook. She pressed her ear to the wood. No one was moving around inside. "Doctor!" she called again.

Her hands stiff with cold, she fumbled in her bag for her lock picks. After a few false starts, the lock gave way, and she found herself in the hallway, dripping dirty water onto the tiles. She tucked the picks back into the bag and closed it. "Dr. Kalderash?"

The thick silence swallowed her voice. The house was still, as only an uninhabited dwelling could be. No one had been there for quite a while, yet the servants' door was open, and light was coming up from below, casting the corridor in soft shadows. Corbeau flattened herself against the doorjamb and listened, but the basement was as silent as the rest of the house.

Suddenly, the front door slammed shut with a bang. Seconds later, she felt the chill in the air and smelled the rain. The back door was open. Locking the front door behind her, she grabbed the lamp from its table, grit crunching under her boots as she made her way toward the back of the house.

The back door stood wide. It hadn't been forced. Careless scratches around the lock told her someone with less skill than she had picked it. Turning the lamp down, she shut this door as well and pulled the bolt. More grit scratched under her boot-soles as she turned. She lifted her lamp to reveal a trail of muddy footprints down the hall. The intruders hadn't bothered to wipe their feet once they'd popped the lock. She knelt down for a closer look. Two sets of muddy boot tracks led from the back door to the front room. Men's tracks. Stout men wearing stout boots. There had been a scuffle near the doorway of the front room. Then they'd doubled back and left the way they'd come.

The house was suffused in an eerie calm that turned the hairs on Corbeau's arms to pins. Something bad had happened here. And whether it had happened as a result of her action, or her failure to act, it was her fault. Forcing herself to breathe, she followed the tracks back down the hall to the front room, where she had, just that morning, interviewed Dr. Kalderash.

She eased the door open, holding the lamp in front of her. Thinking better of it, she set the lamp back on its stand in the hallway and turned it off. Thick curtains hung over the front window, but Corbeau didn't want to risk accidentally shedding light beneath them or through a gap. Instead, she took her tinderbox from her coat pocket, lit her candle stub, and slipped inside.

The front room was a disaster. Even in the flickering light of her candle, she could feel the echoes of violence in the overturned chairs in which she and Dr. Kalderash had sat that morning, the shattered end table where she had set her teacup. The papers once stacked on the desk near the window had been swept to the floor, scattered, and stomped with heavy boots that sullied the delicate rows of handwriting with mud. More papers, journals, and even books had been heaped into the fireplace in such quantity they'd smothered the fire. Only the acrid traces of paper-smoke lingered in the air to evidence a flame had once burned there. The silver samovar lay scratched and dented on the floor beside shards of the teapot and cups Corbeau had drunk from, amid a pool of cold, brown muck.

The intruders had been searching for something. They'd been angry—very angry—when they hadn't found it. But who were they? And what had they been looking for? She wished she'd had a closer look at Dr. Kalderash's papers when she'd been there earlier that day. Now it was too late. What hadn't been obliterated was a jumbled mess that would take hours to sort out.

Had Dr. Kalderash been there to witness the destruction of her study? Had she fled when she'd heard the *scritch-scratch* of the picks in the back door? Or had the intruders taken her unawares? Corbeau shuddered at the thought of how a pair of large, angry men might take out their frustrations on the petite inventor.

She took a deep breath and closed the door behind her.

The footprints in the corridor told a story of struggle that had been fought, fiercely, just before the servants' door. The door had been closed when Corbeau had been there that morning. It was ajar now, and no one had bothered to turn off the lights below. Kalderash had been in the basement when the intruders arrived— had been there, or had run down there after they arrived. They had dragged her up. Corbeau listened at the staircase again, but not even the air stirred in the depths. She snuffed her candle, put it back in her pocket, and followed the light down the stairs.

A soft wall of heat hit her face as she stepped off the last step. The wall lamps were blazing. She turned them down. Dr. Kalderash would not have left the gas on, had she merely gone out. She wouldn't have let the brazier continue to burn, either. After ascertaining that the coals were hiding no important evidence, she doused them with the water from the washbasin that sat beside it on the table. The table that held the brazier and washbasin also held a soup bowl, a single set of cutlery, and a dry end of bread— so much for the kitchen that would normally be housed below stairs. The rest of the basement was given over to machines. She ran her hand over an iron torso cage with a small, locking box welded to the side. What looked like the study of a hand in metal sat near a pile of bolts, springs, and fabric. So many ideas left unfinished. It was as if the inventor had known she didn't have much time and had tried to bring as many of her ideas to life as she could before…before what? Before fleeing the country? Before someone came for her?

The idea was unthinkably sad, but Corbeau forced the sentiment away and returned her attention to the crime scene. The clutter on the table farthest from the stairs was typical work debris—the residue of a quick mind occupied with higher things than tidiness. But closer to the doorway she found more evidence of a fight. They'd come upon Kalderash quickly, while she was close to the door and before she could escape either up the stairs or to the opposite side of the room. Metal scraps littered the floor there, scattered in all directions. And, bringing the lamp close, Corbeau could make out a woman's faint footprint on the wall. Corbeau bit back a smile. Maria Kalderash hadn't gone quietly.

Had the intruders come looking for the inventor herself, or for some object in her possession? The basement had been spared the search and destruction the front room had suffered. Yet one would think if the inventor were downstairs immersed in her work, the intruders would have searched the house quietly, rather than giving her notice and time to escape. Chances were later they'd have their hands too full with Dr. Kalderash to search the basement. What had the intruders been after? Why had they thought it even better to abscond with Dr. Kalderash? Where had they gone, and what had they done with her after that?

Corbeau could think of two people who might have taken her: Prefect Javert and Hermine Boucher. Hermine wanted her lover back. More importantly, if Sophie's story were to be believed—and Corbeau wasn't certain that it was—Madame Boucher needed Dr. Kalderash's assistance suppressing her unwanted supernatural talents. Why Javert wanted the inventor, Corbeau could only speculate. But he wanted her badly enough to frame her for a crime that had never happened.

Corbeau turned to go back up the stairs. She was about to switch off the wall lamps when something in the rubble caught her eye. Crouching down, she extracted an elaborate pince-nez from the debris. She blew off the dust and held the instrument up to the light.

The lenses were glass, like normal lenses. However, instead of being flat, they were convex on both sides, making them almost spherical. A golden mesh was fused to the back side of the lenses. Corbeau frowned. She'd seen the mesh somewhere before. Grasping the spectacles by the bridge, she held them up to her face. Suddenly the instrument leaped toward her eyes as if drawn by a powerful magnet. A current crackled over her skin with a hail of blue sparks. Yelping, she clawed them off. They fell to the floor with a clatter. Could this have been the object the intruders were hunting? Corbeau doubted it. They'd likely been sitting on the table in plain sight before the struggle had buried them. All the same, something told her it would be best for the object to not fall into the wrong hands.

She poked at the spectacles with the toe of her boot. When they didn't bite, she used a rag to pick them up again. The spectacles had seemed to take on a life of their own—as if they had been seeking connection with her skin. That was it, exactly, she realized, her pulse beginning to race with the excitement of discovery. The first time she had seen the mesh was on Armand Lambert's torso. She'd have bet money that, at one time, he had used one of Kalderash's devices. The mesh was probably how the devices connected to the body. But what was the nature of the connection? She didn't have time to speculate now. She knotted the rag tightly around the spectacles and tucked the bundle into her shoulder bag for later examination.

After giving the laboratory a final glance, she extinguished the lights and made her way up the staircase. Back in the corridor, she lit the lamp on the stand near the front door, holding it out in front of her as she followed the footsteps down the hallway toward the rear of the house. The intruders had definitely carried her this way. Closer examination revealed a toe scuff along the wall, a hairpin, and what might well have been a light spatter of blood. Everything stopped abruptly just before the back door. They had subdued her, then, it seemed, and wrestled her outside, not bothering to shut the door behind them. Standing in the doorway, Corbeau looked out.

The rear of the house opened into an alley, where the footprints disappeared into a mess of mud and water spreading out in both directions. Using her hand to shield the lamp from the rain, Corbeau looked up and down the alley. No street-level windows faced out from the adjacent houses, and only a few on the top floor of the adjoining buildings. These remained firmly shuttered and would probably have been shuttered when Kalderash had been taken. Between this, the pouring rain, and the natural inclination of city-dwellers to see and hear nothing that might come back to haunt them later, Corbeau doubted she'd get a word out of the neighbors. Stepping inside again, she locked the door once more.

It was then she noticed a second staircase, with more signs of disturbance leading up to the next floor. The stairs were narrow. Corbeau's shoulders nearly brushed the plaster on either side, and the wood creaked in protest of her every step. A thick crimson-hued Persian carpet lay over the worn planks of the landing. On the other side of it was a single door—the one space, Corbeau speculated, Kalderash had designated for her personal comfort.

The room was cramped, with a steeply pitched ceiling that followed the roofline down toward the street. A single bed sat against the back wall, and next to it, a small bedside table with a book. On the far wall—if anything in this chamber could be considered far from anything else—a round window looked out over the street. A modest wardrobe stood beside it, and on the other side of the wall, a low chest of drawers.

Some struggle had occurred here, as well, though it hadn't been as intense as the battle of the basement. The top two drawers were open, their contents slopped over the sides. The bedclothes hung down over one side of the bed, and a chair was overturned. But the little attic had somehow escaped the wholesale destruction visited upon the front room. Any search had been cursory, secondary to the chase. Had Kalderash escaped her captors and run upstairs? Given two hulking intruders and one delicate inventor, Corbeau doubted it.

No. There had to have been a second abductee.

Corbeau righted the chair and turned toward the bed. The blankets had been pulled down hastily, and she could see the indentations Dr. Kalderash's small bones had made in the mattress. She averted her eyes from this unintentional intimacy, forcing her thoughts back to the scene. The second person had hidden under the bed. Though that person was long gone, he—or she—might have left something behind. Corbeau knelt, pushed the covers away, and set her lamp on the floor. Something was there, back toward the wall, amid the dust. She flattened herself on the floor and eased beneath the bed, tickling at the object with her fingers until she found it. Sighing, she emerged with a brown cloth cap.

"Joseph?"

It was the boy's cap, she was certain of it—from the frayed spot on the brim to the medal of St. Christopher that he always wore on the band. The patron saint of children and travelers. Corbeau had given it to him herself.

She slumped against the bed.

What had Joseph been doing there?

Joseph had a new leg. Dr. Kalderash was in the business of making prosthetics. The Church of the Divine Spark concentrated its healing work in the slums, like the Montagne Ste. Geneviève. What had Joseph said about his flashy new apparatus? That it, and his shoes, had been a reward for a job well done? Joseph was an enterprising kid. Corbeau probably wasn't the only one who employed him as a messenger. Damn. She let out a long, wretched breath, thinking of the trouble she could have saved herself if she'd only pressed Joseph a little harder about his new limb.

Who the devil would have taken both Kalderash and Joseph? They had come to the house seeking something completely different. But what?

Corbeau heaved herself to her feet. Bit by bit, she began to put the room back together, searching for clues as she went. She folded the clothing on the floor and stacked it on the bed. She righted the overturned washstand and set the basin back in place. The wardrobe was unlocked but intact. Inside, the inventor's few dresses hung neatly, with two pairs of shoes in a row on the bottom. Next to the wardrobe, half-concealed beneath a dressing gown near the chest of drawers, was Javert's umbrella, of all improbable things. The silk was torn in two places and several of the baleen ribs had snapped. She smiled briefly, thinking of Joseph clouting his attacker over the head with it. At least she hoped that's what happened.

But she was really interested in the wardrobe. It would look uninteresting to the casual eye, but Corbeau had hidden her share of contraband. Uninteresting places were the best, and a wardrobe lent itself to hiding in more ways than one. She pushed the thin selection of dresses to one side and knocked on the back panel, then along the bottom. There were no false compartments, no sliding panels. She ran her hand along the underside. Still nothing. Sighing, she put a shoulder to the side of the wardrobe and shoved it away from the wall, smiling as her fingers found the evidence she was looking for. "There you are."

Someone had glued a large piece of paper to the back of the wardrobe—that day, Corbeau guessed; the line of glue was still liquid in some places. There was another, larger sheet folded into quarters beneath it. Kneeling down, Corbeau slipped a finger beneath the paper and carefully lifted it away. Then she teased out the lump it had concealed.

She unfolded the paper and spread it out on the floor, to reveal a set of schematics for some kind of device. Sketches showed a flexible tube that fit over a person's arm. Smaller devices were embedded between the layers of the sleeve and connected to one another with wires. Notes accompanied the sketches, written in a tight, small hand. Corbeau squinted at the words until they swam before her eyes. For a moment, she considered giving the strange spectacles another chance. Then she realized she couldn't read the text because not all of it was in French.

It was only when she came to the bottom right-hand corner of the drawing that she found words she recognized. There, in a clear French hand, which stood out from the foreign text like a shining beacon, were the words LEFT HAND OF JUSTICE. Beneath it were two signatures: one, which she could make out as Dr. M. Kalderash, and the other, as clear as day: Claude Javert. And then PROPERTY OF THE DEPARTMENT OF THE UNEXPLAINED, OFFICE OF THE PREFECT OF POLICE.

It was dated the previous year.

So that was why Dr. Kalderash had been so frightened when Corbeau had knocked on her door. She'd thought that Javert had sent her. And she'd been correct. There was a stamp in the lower right-hand corner of the schematics, right below the signatures. The bell, book, and candle were configured differently from the insignia that Corbeau wore, but it was easy to see how someone might confuse them.

Corbeau quickly folded the document and stuffed it into her bag. Her heart pounded. What was the Left Hand of Justice, and why was Javert so desperate to get the plans back? The name suggested police applications. Was it a weapon? That would explain a lot. And what was the Department of the Unexplained? Why had Vidocq never mentioned it? Hadn't Sophie said something about Javert wanting to put the Bureau of Supernatural

Investigations back together? What did she know? And did the Left Hand actually exist, or only in the minds of its creators?

Corbeau took out the documents Javert had given her that morning and glanced at the date on the schematics. At the time Kalderash and Javert had drawn up the plans, Kalderash had been in the country for about a year. She and Hermine Boucher were together for almost that long, which meant these plans had come into existence just before Dr. Kalderash had left Javert's employ and gone to work with Madame Boucher.

Perhaps the people who had taken Dr. Kalderash and Joseph had been looking for these plans. Unable to find them, they had come upon Dr. Kalderash and thought the plan's author was better than the plan itself.

But who? Who had done this thing?

Her thoughts kept returning to Javert. But Javert seemed to be going out of his way to bring Kalderash in by the book. It seemed unlikely that having gone to the bother of asking Corbeau to build a case, he would order a messy kidnapping. No. Javert wasn't that impatient. And he wouldn't draw attention to himself that way.

*Because he was hiding something*, she realized.

The prefect of police was a direct employee of the King, and the King was a reactionary zealot. If Javert was reassembling an organization to address the supernatural, he wouldn't want the King to know about it.

She remembered what the Conciergerie guard had said about a burglary some nights ago. Had Kalderash broken in to Javert's offices to take her plans back? Javert wouldn't risk raising the eyebrows of either the papers or his superiors with some not-quite-legal arrest. Nor could he legitimately go after Dr. Kalderash for burglary without exposing what he was doing. He needed an unrelated excuse to arrest her, even if she was innocent of the crime.

Corbeau began to pace the length of the room. If Javert hadn't taken Dr. Kalderash, there was a good chance Hermine Boucher had. Not only had Dr. Kalderash left their relationship unresolved, according to Sophie, but Dr. Kalderash had herself said that the goal of Madame Boucher's organization was to "expel demons." Had Hermine known about the Left Hand? Might she have seen it as a way to further her calling?

Thunder cracked through the air. Rain battered the roof above and the streets below. The air was cold, damp, and suffused with the metallic smell of the storm. There was a third option, Corbeau realized, her blood running cold. Madame Boucher was no longer the Great Prophet of the Church of the Divine Spark.

That position now belonged to Chief Inspector Vautrin.

When he'd surprised her in the carriage house, she hadn't been able to imagine why the man would involve himself with an organization like the Church of the Divine Spark. But something in what Sophie had said brought all the pieces together.

The Church of the Divine Spark, like the Catholic Church, viewed supernatural phenomena as demonic activity. While Madame Boucher had taken a humanitarian approach, treating the afflicted poor, Vautrin—social climber and frustrated priest—had seen an opportunity to amass power. Worming his way into the core of the organization, he'd watched and waited. When Madame Boucher, the Great Prophet, had pulled her disappearing act, Vautrin had pounced. Whether Madame Boucher would have agreed or not, Vautrin now sat at the head of the Church of the Divine Spark.

And if the Left Hand of Justice was a spiritual weapon of some sort, Corbeau was certain he would stop at nothing to possess it.

She had to speak to Javert, and quickly. He had lied to her and built up a false case against an innocent woman. But if Vautrin had Joseph and Dr. Kalderash, it would take more than one disgraced Sûreté agent to rescue them.

She put the chest of drawers back together, taking the time to search for false bottoms, extra panels, and anything else that might have been of interest. Her cheeks burned as she folded the inventor's silky underthings and placed them back in their drawers. Someone else had gone through them before Corbeau had arrived, but perhaps feeling the same embarrassment they hadn't done more than dump out the drawers.

It was in the bottom drawer, which impatient hands had only examined in the most cursory way, that she found the other piece of the puzzle. There, sandwiched between folds of silk and cotton, was a length of folded fabric that glinted in the low light of the lamp. Corbeau brought it out and laid it open on the carpet. It was a tightly woven golden mesh, as thin and gossamer-light as spider-silk—the same as was fused to the back of the spectacles, embedded in Lambert's torso, and very likely attached to Joseph's new foot. As she ran her hand across it, the metal warmed and sucked at her skin, while her fingers raised delicate sparks as they traveled across it.

Corbeau's thoughts turned back to the schematics for the Left Hand of Justice. There had been a sleeve, a flexible sleeve that fit over the arm. Could the metal fabric be meant for this? It would make sense, given that Kalderash had hidden the schematics not far away. Corbeau smiled. Considering many men's squeamishness about feminine necessities, the lingerie drawer had been an excellent hiding place. She refolded the cloth and carefully tucked it into her bag as well. She shut the drawers and sat back down on the bed to think. Dr. Kalderash and Joseph were in trouble and needed her help. But she had no idea where to find them. What she did have, though, was something that Javert was after—something with which she could compel him to assist her in finding them. That was just what she intended to do.

And she'd take him his damned umbrella back while she was at it.

## CHAPTER ELEVEN

Claude Javert, Prefect of Police, kept his lair amid the narrow, winding streets around the new Lycée Charlemagne, the grounds of which had once been home to the Jesuit order from whence he emerged. Conveniently, both the house and the Lycée were situated almost equidistant from Javert's current offices at the Conciergerie and the home of his quarry on the Rue des Rosiers.

Javert's home comprised the second and third floors above a milliner's shop on the Rue St. Paul. The shop's large front window was dark, the milliner's extravagant creations casting weird shadows in the light of a nearby streetlamp. The apartments above rose from the wooden shop front in an orderly configuration of light-gray stone, tall windows, and black iron balconies. The street was hardly wide enough for three people to walk abreast, but it was quiet, evenly paved, and clear of debris.

The Conciergerie clock struck half past ten as Corbeau approached the building. The first row of windows above the milliner's shop was dark, though a light burned in one of the front rooms on the third floor. It was admittedly a little late for calling, but this wasn't a social visit. With any luck, Corbeau would soon have Javert's admission that he'd sent her on a false errand and his subsequent promise of assistance. He might even be able to give her a hint about who else was after the Left Hand of Justice, and where they might be keeping Dr. Kalderash and Joseph. She ducked inside the door next to the milliner's and ascended a dark staircase. At the top of the stairs she knocked at his door.

The last time she had seen the prefect, in the cramped darkness of his carriage, in the small, dark hours and pouring rain, he had been an imposing sight. Now, in his dressing gown and slippers, he seemed diminished. His shoulders were thin beneath the robe and pajamas, and the sparse hair on his chest was gray.

"Inspector!" he said warmly, though he couldn't hide his surprise.

"I tried to find you earlier at your office, but—"

"Oh, yes. I heard about that. I was out of the building at the time." Brightening, he said, "I assume you couldn't wait another moment to start on that arrest warrant. Do come inside."

He led her to what would have been a parlor in another home. Here, the room resembled what she imagined his office must look like. A desk dominated the small chamber, papers stacked neatly beside the blotter, an oil lamp turned up bright enough for work. Bookshelves lined the walls. He had set his writing instrument down on the blotter near the ink bottle when her knock had sounded. As he ushered her in, he took it up again and replaced the cap.

"May I?" she asked.

"Please." He handed it to her. "It was a gift from the head of my order."

"The Jesuits?"

He graced her with an evasive smile. "It has an internal ink reservoir. It's one of the few of its kind in existence. The French government has just patented the design."

She turned the instrument over in her hands, admiring the ruby-tipped gold nib. The barrel had been lovingly carved from a dark, exotic wood that felt both solid and silky beneath her fingers. It had likely cost what she'd make in two years. Reluctantly, she handed the pen back to him. He gestured toward two chairs that sat before the desk, taking the other after she was settled.

His parlor was a masculine room, all wood, straight lines, and business. But a framed portrait of a woman hung over the fireplace, and below it, a sprinkling of gold-touched statuettes spread over the mantel.

"My wife," Javert said, following her eyes.

She was a pleasant-looking woman, some years younger at the time of the portrait than Javert was now. She had a plump, smiling face and eyes that danced with a lively intelligence. Corbeau wasn't sure which surprised her more: that Javert had a wife or that she would appear both comely and kind. "Congratulations."

"Where are my manners? May I take your coat?"

The damp wool fell away as he eased the garment off her shoulders, and the warmth of the fire crackling in the fireplace surrounded her like a gentle cocoon. Javert laid the coat across the back of his own chair.

"Trousers," Javert remarked, taking in her borrowed clothing. "I've never understood why women insist on such ridiculous excesses when it comes to dress. Corsets, bustles, all that boning—it seems contrary to nature. And to movement itself. This suits you."

"It would suit a lot of women. But as a priest, you know how much energy the Church puts into suppressing both women's nature and our movements. Fashion both restrains a woman and makes her decorative."

Javert nodded. "Point taken, Inspector. Perhaps one day you'll be in a position to do something about it. Won't you sit down? Now, about that arrest warrant." He turned, took a stack of papers from the desk, and began to leaf through them, as if he had the document already drawn up and waiting—which, knowing him, he probably did.

"Actually, the situation has changed." Corbeau reached into her shoulder bag, fingers tingling as they brushed the tightly rolled metal mesh. She pushed it aside, found the sleeve she'd taken from Madame Boucher's dress, and laid it across her knee. "You do recognize this."

Javert's eyes went wide as he registered the fabric of the garment, the cut of the sleeve, and the distinctive beadwork of the dress Hermine Boucher had been wearing the night of her disappearance. "Where—where did you find it?"

"The question is, why didn't you find it? If your men had so much as glanced inside Madame Boucher's carriage, they wouldn't have been able to miss it. Here's your umbrella back, by the way." He didn't protest as she pressed the broken mass of silk and baleen into his hand. Rather, he continued to stare at the sleeve as if it were a specter. "It was stuffed inside the seat cushion of the carriage. No one kidnapped Madame Boucher, Monsieur. She disappeared of her own accord, with the assistance of three servants, one of whom the chief inspector took into custody this morning." When he remained silent, she added, "If that wasn't enough, your favorite suspect was herself kidnapped earlier today. It's inconvenient, I know."

Javert swallowed. Blinked. A clock on the bookshelf softly chimed the quarter hour. "This is an interesting development."

"I thought you might think so. Since your goal all along was to apprehend Dr. Kalderash rather than to recover Madame Boucher, I thought you might be behind it. But you wouldn't draw attention to your side projects by banging down an innocent person's door in the middle of the day."

"My side projects?" Javert had regained some of his composure, but not enough to be convincing.

"Does the Left Hand of Justice sound familiar? Or perhaps the Department of the Unexplained?"

To his credit, the prefect didn't blanch or panic. Instead, he heaved a great sigh, running a hand over his face as if he were very, very tired. "Inspector, you look as ragged as I feel. Would you care to discuss this over a spot of late supper?"

Without waiting for an answer, he left the room and returned shortly with a tray of bread, meat, cheese, and sliced apples. He set the tray on the table, along with plates, glasses, and a bottle of rather nice red wine. Corbeau's stomach growled. She hesitated but, when he insisted, began to fill her plate while he poured the wine.

"You found the plans, then, when you were interviewing Dr. Kalderash," Javert said. Corbeau didn't answer. Instead, she bit off an inelegant mouthful of light, crusty bread that couldn't have been older than that morning and washed it down with wine. "She stole them from me."

"I know."

"I can't emphasize how important it is that I recover those designs."

"Important enough to arrest an innocent woman for a crime that didn't happen?"

"There was always the chance," he said weakly.

"A chance that would have disintegrated like wet paper if you'd bothered to examine the situation a little more deeply."

Javert sighed again, shoulders slumping, and dropped his head. Corbeau almost felt sorry for him. "I wasn't intending to hold her forever. Those plans are property of the Office of the Prefect. She stole them." He narrowed his eyes. "Where did you say you found them?"

"I didn't say I found them."

"Did you also find the device? Has she completed a prototype?"

"I don't know." Corbeau sat back in her chair, regarding him thoughtfully as she swirled the wine around the bulb of her glass. The wine was viscous, a sign of quality, and clung in an even film to the side of the glass. Rare pens, two floors on the Rue St. Paul, and fine wine to serve up to an unexpected guest—where was the money coming from? "How long did you and Dr. Kalderash work together?"

"A little more than a year. Her research had come to my attention some time before that. We corresponded for several years, during which time I tried to convince her to come to Paris. She wouldn't. You'd think her type wouldn't mind pulling up stakes, but she claimed to be happy in her village, building better pitchforks and whatnot. Eventually, fortuitous events conspired to bring her to Paris." Corbeau cocked an eyebrow. "Religious hysteria swept through her part of the country. Claiming she was a witch, her neighbors burned her out of house and home. An all-too-familiar story, but I don't have to tell you that."

The slice of apple Corbeau was eating turned to sawdust in her mouth. "You call that fortuitous?"

"It was for me. I smuggled her into Paris and brought her to work for the Department of the Unexplained. Her inventions funded the department almost entirely."

"What happened?"

He considered her carefully. "We had a difference of opinion."

"You meant the Left Hand of Justice to be a weapon. She disagreed."

He bowed his head. "The plans are the property of the department. She had no right to take them. Do you have them with you?"

"They're safe," Corbeau said.

He tore off a piece of bread with his teeth, chewing slowly. "You're not just going to hand them over."

"Tell me about the metal fabric."

He regarded her for one long, piercing moment. Then he said, "You looked at the schematics."

"It is for the sleeve, then." Javert made an affirmative noise. "It must have cost more than your fancy pen. Why not something cheaper, like cotton?"

The mesh somehow enabled Kalderash's devices to connect to the body—this Corbeau knew. But it was the nature of the connection that she wanted to understand.

Javert set his glass down hard on the desk. "Inspector, we don't have time for this. For all I know, that woman has built the thing already. She could be trying to sell it to one of the many, many enemies of the King. Or to a foreign government. I don't know if you understand precisely what could happen if she did."

"There is no prototype."

"How do you know?"

Corbeau didn't know, of course. But all things considered, it made sense. That length of spun, woven metal had not been intended for practice, and Corbeau hadn't found anything on the premises that might have been.

"The piece of fabric I found was uncut. As expensive as it must have been, she wouldn't have commissioned much more than she needed. She'd have used something cheaper to get the fit and proportions right. I searched her rooms thoroughly and didn't find anything like that."

Relaxing a bit, Javert refilled his glass. "You may be right," he admitted. "So what do you propose to do?"

"Me?"

"That's why you're here, isn't it?"

"I'm here to stop you from pursuing Dr. Kalderash as a criminal and to ask your assistance finding her—and Joseph, a young boy in her employ who was taken along with her."

Javert pursed his lips. He downed the contents of his glass and set it back on the desk. He clearly wasn't happy with the direction the conversation was taking.

But if she had to, she could compel his assistance. "Who else is after them? Besides you, of course." Javert's brows drew tight. He hadn't considered the idea, clearly, and now that he had, his conclusions disturbed him. "The people who took Dr. Kalderash and Joseph were looking for something. I'm willing to bet that they were after the plans as well. Who do you think it was? Vautrin? Now that he's wormed his way to the head of Madame Boucher's organization, I'm sure he'd have a lot of use for something like that."

"Vautrin? How—"

"How did I know Vautrin was involved? Don't insult us both, Monsieur."

Javert closed his eyes and sighed again. "Good God. Vautrin and the Left Hand of Justice. The very thought of it." A thought he hadn't considered, Corbeau realized from his reaction. "Are you certain he knows about it?"

"Let's think about this. Dr. Kalderash fled the Bureau of the Unexplained and flew straight into Madame Boucher's arms. There would have been some pillow talk, I'm sure." She glanced again at the portrait above the mantel. "Even you don't keep everything from your wife. Vautrin rises to the inner circle—they're calling him the Great Prophet now, you know. Don't you think someone would tell the Great Prophet about the new weapon that's going to help the Divine Spark rid the world of demons?"

"God." He ran his hand over his face again, shaking his head. When he spoke, his voice sounded exhausted and old. "Vautrin can't get his hands on this technology. Even you can see this, Inspector."

"He doesn't have it. But he may have Dr. Kalderash. You're going to help me get her back."

"And then you'll give me the plans."

She finished her wine in one long pull. "If you help me find Dr. Kalderash and Joseph, get them to safety, and drop the charges against Dr. Kalderash, I'll make sure your superiors never know that you and Dr. Kalderash were going into the business of making supernatural weapons." His eyes flashed dangerously. Corbeau set her glass on the desk. "Or I could take everything I know to the Ministry of the Interior, including the fact that the chief inspector holds a high position in a heretical—perhaps even revolutionarily inclined group—a fact of which you have had full knowledge for some time, but have done nothing about."

His long, strong fingers clenched the arm of his chair. If he'd had a dagger at hand, it would have been sticking out of her eye by that point—facts that only convinced Corbeau the risk she was taking was both necessary and right. He seethed. "Those plans belong to me."

"Or perhaps you'd prefer Hermine Boucher get ahold of them. I noticed you omitted reference to her little club when you enlisted my help finding Kalderash."

"I was hoping to protect you."

"You were hoping to protect yourself. Tell me, Monsieur, where do you stand on the forceful suppression of supernatural energies?" When he remained silent, she said, "It's not important. What is important is that these fanatics, either under Madame Boucher's command or Vautrin's, have taken an innocent woman and a little boy. It's going to take more than me to affect a rescue. That's where your help comes in."

"You seem to have this all figured out."

"I'm just doing my job," Corbeau said.

Javert smiled hatefully. "Speaking of your job, blackmailing the prefect of police is not going to get it back for you."

Corbeau's stomach clenched. That was why she'd taken the case in the first place. She'd lost sight of that fact. But her ambition wasn't important anymore. There was too much at stake, and too much innocent blood on her hands already. "At this point, Monsieur, I'm more concerned about justice."

"God help us all."

"Which reminds me, you were right when you said you thought the Montagne Ste. Geneviève incidents were related. The three victims—Lambert, Fournier, and Bertrand—all worked for Madame Boucher. They were the ones who helped her disappear. At the time of their outbursts, they had all been taking a preparation meant to suppress flares of spiritual energy. And they had all been running from something."

"Someone's covering their tracks," Javert said.

"That was my thought. My money's on Vautrin. He stood to benefit from everyone believing Madame Boucher had been taken, but more importantly, from her staying gone. I don't suppose you have any news about Armand Lambert?"

"Lambert...Ah, yes, you asked me about him earlier." Javert closed his eyes and shook his head. "They found his body this afternoon. It wasn't a natural death."

"Vautrin." Corbeau let out a long breath and sat back in her chair. Several moments ticked past on the clock on the bookshelf. The air had gone from comforting warmth to stifling. She pulled at her collar. "How long have you known about his involvement?"

"I planted him there a year ago. I thought it would be useful to have someone keeping an eye on Dr. Kalderash." Corbeau stared. The thought of someone deliberately putting that poisonous man anywhere near Maria Kalderash made her blood boil. "He did that, but he also…developed ideas of his own."

"And you didn't pull him immediately?"

"I was watching him. Though at the time I couldn't imagine… he's such a stickler for religious law."

"Which includes the Church's position on supernatural phenomena. He may have gone in with the best intentions," Corbeau said, "but when he saw an opportunity to further his religious agenda, he grabbed it with both hands."

"God, what a mess." He tipped the bottle over his glass, but all that proceeded from it was a few sediment-laden drops. He set the bottle aside. "You never did tell me what you were doing at Madame Boucher's house this evening."

"It's an interesting story. The Divine Spark offered me a job."

"Oh?"

"Vautrin is taking the group's good works to the world. They intend to create medicines to suppress supernatural energy on a large scale."

"They needed an alchemist," Javert said. Corbeau nodded. "But did Vautrin really seek you out for this position?"

Corbeau laughed. "Vautrin can't stand working with me even in a legal capacity. He sure wouldn't willingly bring me into some organization he was intending to take over."

"Then who? Vidocq went to such lengths to destroy your criminal records and set you up with a new identity. Who else knew?"

Corbeau glanced at her glass then looked away. "There was…someone," she eventually said. "Someone who, it appears, believes in the movement and genuinely wanted to bring me in. Someone who thinks that suppressing these natural energies on a large scale is a desirable thing, and that I, too, would believe in the cause once I understood what they were trying to do."

Javert cocked an eyebrow. "What's her name?"

Now it was Corbeau's turn to look away. Clearly her disastrous personal life was not as closely kept as she'd endeavored. And yet, what an astonishing lack of judgment had been in his voice. He seemed to be disappointed rather than shocked, and more disappointed in the fact of her professional lapse than in anything else.

"It seems we're both at fault in this situation, Monsieur," she said, the fatigue in her voice now matching that in his. She met his eyes. "Will you help me?"

"Do I have any choice?"

"You have the choice between doing the right thing and making this a lot harder and a lot more unpleasant than it has to be."

He cocked his head, regarding her with a mix of resignation and admiration. Then he nodded. "Very well, Inspector. Where do we start?"

# CHAPTER TWELVE

By the time Corbeau departed Javert's tidy rooms above the haberdashery, the prefect had promised not only to send a handful of his best to meet her at Madame Boucher's mansion, but also to have them detain Chief Inspector Vautrin, if they found him. Corbeau wasn't certain Joseph and Dr. Kalderash were actually at the mansion. If they were, she had been close enough to rescue them herself just a few hours ago. The thought made her grind her teeth. On the other hand, if they were being held somewhere else, Corbeau would be back where she had started nearly twenty-four hours before—nowhere. No, not even *there*. At least when Javert's carriage had discharged her onto the pavement in front of Oubliette, she'd had an address and a suspect.

The haberdashery disappearing behind her, she followed the street past the Rue Charlemagne, where His Majesty had founded the new Lycée less than a decade before. Buildings of white and brown stone rose up on either side of the narrow lane-like canyon walls, magnifying the echo of her hurried footfall against the slick cobblestones. The air was thick with the smell of rain, and moisture formed halos around the well-kept gaslights, but at least for now the precipitation had stopped.

As the Rue St. Paul approached the Seine, it angled slightly downward before flinging itself wide onto a bustling nighttime market. Corbeau stopped to adjust her appearance. The borrowed shirt and trousers felt good against her skin. Not only were they clean, but they provided a freedom of movement she had been sorely missing. She pulled her bag closer and tucked her hair up under the cloth cap that had come with the trousers and shirt. She bent down and scooped up a bit of mud from between the cobblestones. Smudging it on her cheeks and hands, she checked her reflection in a darkened shop window and nodded satisfaction. The suggestion of disguise wouldn't hold up to close scrutiny, but it should be enough to allow her to walk the crowded street unquestioned and unmolested. Her height and build would strengthen the illusion; darkness would perfect it. She took a deep breath and stepped into the throng.

A lively traffic carried her along the street, as energetic an hour before midnight as in the middle of the day. All along the riverside, customers haggled with merchants in slapdash stalls and over the sides of boats pulled up to the quay for just that purpose. Corbeau caught the whiff of chestnuts roasting on a brazier and, below that, the mingled smells of spilled beer, tobacco, and sewage. Strains of a violin darted in and out of the sounds of lapping water and commerce.

Lambert was dead. Vautrin had killed him, most likely to keep him silent regarding the truth about Madame Boucher's disappearance. But why had Madame Boucher done her disappearing act in the first place? Had she endeavored to bring sympathy to her cause? Or perhaps she had learned of Vautrin's ambitions and feared them? Had she known that her disappearance would cast suspicion on her former lover? If Javert hadn't wanted Dr. Kalderash for his own purposes, the newspapers and police would have only been too happy to take up the cause. Or perhaps this had been Madame's purpose all along—some kind of twisted revenge against Dr. Kalderash for leaving? Corbeau cursed, causing the people walking in front of her to glance her way and move aside.

Stepping past them, she turned her thoughts to Dr. Kalderash. The inventor had cited violent jealousy as her reason for leaving

Madame Boucher's milieu. It certainly seemed possible. But it could also be just one part of the truth. The more she thought about it, the more she was sure that Kalderash had told Madame Boucher about the Left Hand of Justice. They had been in love—Kalderash had been adamant about that. And Kalderash had been running from Javert. Lovers could be mind-bogglingly indiscreet, especially in that first, heady rush of emotion, when the object of one's affection seems unassailably perfect and the end of love is inconceivable. Of course Kalderash had told her rescuer what she was hiding and why. The question was, what did Madame Boucher do with the information?

If Madame Boucher really had been on a crusade, she had to have known that, at some point, she would encounter resistance. She had to have seen the potential for a weapon like the Left Hand of Justice. Perhaps this potential, rather than simple jealousy, had precipitated Dr. Kalderash's departure—just as it had precipitated her departure from the Department of the Unexplained. Now, if she could just figure out at what point Vautrin had decided to step out of his role as Javert's informant and start down the road of his own dark ambitions.

The crowd seemed suddenly, unbearably close. Rain and night had cleansed the air, but she choked on it all the same. She pushed her way out of the crowd, heart racing, and leaned against the corner of a building, elbows on knees. Eventually the sensation passed and she rose, drawing a long, cool breath.

"We meet again, Inspector." Corbeau whirled, but before she could put a face to the gravelly voice behind her, a thick arm coiled around her neck, while another snaked through her elbows, pinning her arms. The voice was familiar, the words hissed through missing teeth. The man sounded pleased. She suddenly recognized the distinctive voice, and her heart sank.

"I've got the money. Tell Jacques—"

"It's too late for that now." The man flexed his arm and pulled her tighter to him, a low chuckle rumbling in his chest. Corbeau gasped for breath. A veil of stars clouded her vision, but in her mind's eye she could see the smug, jowly, pockmarked face of the man she'd left bleeding on the floor of Oubliette the night before.

"Get someone to stitch your face up?" Her voice came out a ragged wheeze. The man chuckled again as he began to drag her back into the alley, her boot heels leaving parallel ruts in the mud. In front of her, the market crowd continued to surge and flow, the people that comprised it blissfully unaware of what was happening in the alley a few short yards away. The shadows closed around them; if anyone had seen her, they didn't see her anymore.

Once out of sight, the man tightened his arm to the point Corbeau was half convinced he was trying to crush her windpipe. But Jacques was a businessman. A dead debtor was not only useless; the body was a liability. But that didn't mean he wouldn't give her something to think about, even if she gave him every last coin in Javert's pouch. She flailed against the man's iron grip, but to no avail. He waited patiently as she continued to struggle and gasp until finally her limbs went heavy, she slumped against him, and the shadows of the alley swallowed them whole.

❖

"Inspector."

Cold water hit her face. Corbeau sputtered and blinked. She tried to move, but her limbs were bound tight. She was tied to a chair. Her cap had come off, and her hair lay plastered to her neck, dripping cold water down the back of her shirt. She struggled against the ropes, pulling side to side until the chair overbalanced and teetered onto two legs. Hands caught the chair and righted it before she hit the ground.

"I apologize for the ropes," Ugly Jacques said. "But they're for your protection. André hasn't quite forgiven you for what you did to him at Oubliette. He's looking for an excuse to finish what you started, and I wouldn't want you to inadvertently give him one."

"Shit," Corbeau said.

Jacques laughed. "Normally, I don't approve of strong language from women, but in your case, I think it's warranted."

They were in a windowless room—a basement, she surmised. The only light was from a lantern, which, from the angle of the shadows, was hanging on the wall behind her. That had to be where the entrance was. Boxes were stacked along one wall, the chair the only furniture. They were under a business, then, or a warehouse. Somewhere that would be closed for the night and abandoned.

"I have the money," she said.

He chuckled and pulled out the pouch Javert had given her, tossing it into the air and catching it. Ugly Jacques wasn't as objectively unattractive as his name led a person to believe. He had the muscles of a laborer and the scarred hands and reshaped nose of a fighter. The nose suited him, though. Without it, his light, wavy hair might have seemed angelic and the twinkle in his blue eye something other than malice.

"This?" he asked, tossing the purse again. "There were a few sous in here, but not nearly what you still owe."

Corbeau craned her neck to glare at André. Now, *André* was ugly—especially when he was jingling her coins in his jacket pocket. Laughing, he spat out a great oyster-like gob, which landed at her feet. Corbeau turned back to her captor.

"He took it," Corbeau said. "Check his coat."

Ugly Jacques laughed again. "And I should believe you because you've dealt so honestly with me so far? Really, Inspector, I'm disappointed. I do you a favor, and this is how you repay me."

"You don't understand!"

Whether he did or not was immaterial, of course. Jacques didn't care why she needed the money. If Joseph and his mother owned their house outright or slept in the streets, it wouldn't make a bit of difference to him. What Jacques did understand was that Corbeau owed him money, and lots of it. As he strode back and forth across the length of the stuffy little room, fingering the knife at his belt, she could almost hear the conflict in his mind. On one hand, the longer she avoided payment, the more interest accrued. On the other hand, no matter how much interest accrued, if he let payment slide, he might not see a penny. As satisfying as it would be to maim, or even kill her, doing either would likewise ensure he would never get his money. Feet shuffled on the dirt behind her. A third man.

Corbeau began to panic. Even if they didn't hurt her badly enough to keep her from crawling out of that basement, eventually, she had to get to Dr. Kalderash and Joseph. And she had to stop Vautrin. She felt someone press up against her back and hoped it wasn't André. Her hopes were scuttled when she felt his soft, rough laugh through the back of her head and his shovel-like hand stroking her throat.

"If you kill me, you'll never get your money," she said.

Ugly Jacques stopped pacing and turned. "It's true. On the other hand, the way prices are rising, by the time you pay me back, it won't be worth anything anyway. And André has put up with so much from you. It's not fair that he not get to have his fun."

Corbeau's heart stopped. They both knew that André had taken the money from Javert's purse. And she was pretty sure they both knew what sort of fun André would have once Jacques and the others left her alone in the basement. Yes, it made sense. Jacques wouldn't endanger her livelihood with a beating. But he would make his position clear; he would assert his masculine authority through André in the time-honored tradition. She began to struggle again, to the great amusement of the hulking beast behind her.

"I can have the money for you in an hour's time." Javert didn't live far. He would give it to her. He had to give it to her.

Ugly Jacques smiled, his teeth unnaturally straight and sharp. "I'm afraid the terms of our agreement have changed."

"Half an hour," she said. "Come with me."

André's cracked, dirty fingertips began to caress her lips. She wanted to bite them, but he could have snapped her neck as easily as swatting a fly. She pulled against the ropes again but stopped when she realized that if she tipped over at this point, it would only make things easier for them. Jacques continued to watch her with the interest of a boy pulling the wings off a fly. He would have been the kind of boy to pull off the legs, too, one by one. A cold drop of perspiration slid down her back. But panic was not the answer.

She calmed her breathing. It would be a mistake to show fear at this point. She steeled her body and began to build a wall around her mind. While Jacques's thug exacted his punishment, her thoughts would be wandering Boucher Mansion, trying to figure out where they were keeping Dr. Kalderash and Joseph.

So deep was she in thought she nearly missed the sudden change in Jacques's demeanor, the furrowed brow, the flick of his hand, and the rush of cool air as André stepped back from her as if burned.

"Of course, now that I think about it, Inspector, it occurs to me that you have something I want even more than money, and even more than revenge."

André's disappointment was palpable.

Corbeau frowned. He *couldn't* mean the Left Hand of Justice. Jacques was the master of his domain, but it was one of petty criminals and small-time vice. Not that he wouldn't love to have a weapon like the Left Hand of Justice at his disposal, but Corbeau knew he didn't have either the connections or the reach. "I'm listening."

"It's not so much a thing as a service." Jacques grew serious. He squatted down to her level, the arrogance leaving his expression. In the light of the lantern behind her, he almost looked human. "You'll forgive my dramatic and heavy-handed manner," he said. Corbeau would forgive him nothing, but curiosity and her instinct for self-preservation ensured she would listen. "I don't have to tell you how late you've been with your payments. And I had to make sure you weren't holding out on me. Business is business." Corbeau met his supplication with a cold stare. He sighed. "I understand that you're investigating the disturbances in Montagne Ste. Geneviève. One of the victims, Claudine Fournier, is very dear to me."

Corbeau blinked. "The fire-starter."

"That's right." Jacques gestured to one of the men standing behind her. The man dragged one of the boxes from beside the wall and positioned it for Jacques to sit. "You tended to her, very kindly, according to witnesses. She woke the next morning as if nothing had happened. But sometime that day, she disappeared."

Disappeared? Corbeau's heart sank. If Vautrin had anything to do with it, Mademoiselle Fournier was already dead. Corbeau just hoped it wouldn't fall to her to break the news to Ugly Jacques. "I'm sorry."

"If you find her, I'd be willing to consider the business between us closed. She is…she is everything to me."

Corbeau blinked again. Who could have guessed that beneath the flashy clothes and layers of cologne beat an actual human heart? A fallible heart whose weakness could be exploited to broker her freedom. Would wonders never cease? "You love her?" she asked.

He nodded. "Can you find her?"

"I don't know."

He sighed, resting his massive, square chin in one hand, elbow on knee. "She works as a paid companion to that woman who disappeared. Boucher. I never liked those people. They gave me the shivers. But Claudine said it was good work, and she didn't mind. Said Madame had even promised to help her with her little problem." He smiled, fleeting and bitter. "Didn't bother me, but she was so ashamed of it."

"Was she taking any sort of preparation to suppress it?"

"Yeah. Yeah, come to think of it, she was."

Corbeau nodded. Just like Lambert. The past was repeating itself, only this time it wasn't her fault. Had anyone heard from Michel Bertrand? She regarded Ugly Jacques gravely. Part of her wanted to promise she'd find his Claudine—promise him anything he wanted, just to get out of there—and let the consequences catch up with her later. But the last twenty-four hours had been nothing if not a lesson in just what a mistake it was to borrow trouble from the future.

"I can't promise to return her alive," she said. "In fact, the odds are against it. There were three victims in the Montagne Ste. Geneviève, and one has turned up dead."

"It's those Divine Spark people, isn't it? Always knew they were no good."

Ironic, Corbeau thought, coming from a man who had just threatened to let his thug recover his debts from her flesh. "I can't tell you the details. It would jeopardize the investigation. But I can assure you that I will personally see the guilty parties punished for their crimes. If someone has harmed Mademoiselle Fournier, they will hang for it, I promise."

He seemed to consider this for a moment, then, pressing his hands to his knees, he stood.

"Untie her. Go on," he said when his men didn't immediately jump to the task. They freed her arms first, then her feet. She stood gingerly, flexing her fingers and toes as the crawling sensation of pins and needles signaled that blood was returning to her extremities. "Tell me honestly. Do you think she's still alive?"

"Possibly."

He looked as happy with the answer as Corbeau felt delivering it. But he knew as well as she did that false hope would get them nowhere. He extended his hand. Corbeau hesitated then took it.

"I'm a businessman, Inspector. My methods can be harsh, but I'm a man of my word. Find my Claudine, alive or dead, and consider your debt repaid in full." Corbeau's eyes went, unbidden, to André's hand jangling the coins in his pocket. André caught her eye and sneered. "In the meantime, if you need anything to aid you in your search, I, and my men, are at your disposal."

Corbeau thought for a moment. "Do you know whether the Divine Spark did all of their work at the house? Or did Claudine mention another place, maybe where they might have done things they wouldn't want the neighbors to find out about?"

Jacques scratched his head, frowning. "There was another place, come to think of it. Not too far from here, actually. Down by the water. Claudine had me fetch her there, now and then, when it was dark. Said the Gypsy woman had a lab there. Noisy business, apparently, but given the neighborhood, nobody ever noticed."

Corbeau's heart beat fast. If the Divine Spark—either Madame Boucher's followers or Vautrin's—were holding Dr. Kalderash for the purpose of bringing the Left Hand of Justice to life, they were holding her there. And chances were, Joseph would be there too. If only she had some way of getting word to Javert! But time was of the essence, and if Vautrin was still at Madame Boucher's house, then Javert's men would do the most good detaining him there. And perhaps, if Claudine Fournier was at the house, they could ensure her safety as well.

"Can you get someone to take me there?" Corbeau asked.

"Certainly."

"Not him." She looked daggers at André.

Jacques's mouth twisted wryly. "No, no, that wouldn't do at all. I'll take you there myself."

"One more thing. Do you know the boy Joseph, who sometimes runs messages for me?"

"I've seen him."

"It's possible that they're holding him, along with Dr. Kalderash and Mademoiselle Fournier. My debt to his family is greater than anything I will ever owe you. If anything happens to him, I would appreciate it if you would promise to watch out for his family."

Jacques nodded, short and quick. "Anything else?"

"Can I have my purse back?"

Clapping her on the back, Ugly Jacques laughed out loud.

## CHAPTER THIRTEEN

Jacques led her through back streets and hidden passages to a tight, dark alley that stank of refuse, stagnant water, and decay. At the mouth of the alley, she hesitated, wondering if she wasn't walking into a trap. But then Jacques stopped, put a finger to his lips, and gestured toward a narrow door. "There it is," he said, stepping back. "Good luck."

Corbeau opened her mouth to thank him, but by the time she'd turned, he had melted back into the shadows. She leaned against the crumbling bricks and evaluated the building on the other side of the alley. It had been a tenement once, possibly a factory. Now it stood dark and abandoned. The windows that weren't boarded up were jagged black holes. Nothing stirred in the alley, though not far away the strains of raucous music and breaking glass marked one of the low taverns that dotted the darker parts of the city. The air was tense with foreboding. Corbeau wasn't surprised Claudine had been afraid to walk home from there. The place was, however, the perfect location for a noisy machine lab or for holding prisoners. Glancing toward the rooftops, then up and down the alley, she darted toward the door that Jacques had indicated. It was locked tight, as she'd expected it would be, but the locks gave way easily to her picks, and she was inside within seconds.

Beyond the door it was as dark as the grave. Her hand instinctively went to her tinderbox. Fortunately, training overruled instinct. Pressing herself up against the wall, she took her hand out of her pocket and waited for her vision to adjust. Ahead of her, at the end of a narrow corridor, she could make out the dim rectangle of a window from the cracks of muted light pushing between the boards that had been nailed unevenly over it. A staircase to her left led up, while another to her right led down. No footsteps creaked overhead, no conversations hummed. However, if she listened hard, she thought she could discern voices below, as well as the soft clank of metal and tools.

Jacques had told her the truth. Dr. Kalderash had once maintained a laboratory in the building. And Corbeau would have bet her own left arm the doctor was working down there at that moment, against her will. Did she have a second set of plans for the Left Hand of Justice? Had she committed the plans to memory? Or was she working blind, without plans or materials, trying to stay alive while she looked for an opportunity to escape?

The basement stairwell was crooked, the railing unsteady. She made her way down slowly, keeping to the wall and walking on the solid edges of the stairs. The stairs ended at a basement corridor, dimly illuminated by a shaft of light that proceeded from beneath a closed door.

"Elise!" a voice hissed.

Corbeau whirled. Sophie stood at the head of the stairs like an apparition. In the light of her candle, Corbeau could make out a loose, white gown, of the type Madame Boucher was said to favor, and soft-soled slippers. She wore her hair free, combed down over her shoulders in a reddish-gold cascade. She looked as if she'd just awakened, which, considering the time, was quite possible.

"Sophie, you scared the life out of me," Corbeau whispered back.

"What are you doing here? Oh!" she exclaimed, as if she'd reached some long-desired conclusion. "This is perfect!" Sophie glided down the stairs, her face alight with pleasant surprise. No, it was stronger than that. She looked as if the impossible dream she'd prayed fervently over had come to life before her eyes.

Corbeau began to caution her to be silent, but before she could form the words, Sophie was already beside her. What's more, she'd made no more noise coming down than her candle. "How did you figure out to come here?"

An inner voice urged her to caution. Sophie had set her up, sent her to the Divine Spark as an alchemist. But she hadn't sent her here; she'd sent her to where Vautrin was. She'd known that Madame Boucher was safe but had sent Corbeau to Vautrin.

"Is Madame Boucher here?" Corbeau asked.

Sophie nodded. "She's downstairs. You figured it out, Elise! Oh, this is too good!"

"And Vautrin?" Sophie's lips pursed at the mention of his name. With guilt, Corbeau guessed. And in the tense moment that followed, Corbeau saw the train of events as clearly as if they had played out before her eyes. Sophie had been angry when Hermine Boucher had wanted Dr. Kalderash back. When Hermine had disappeared, Sophie had quietly thrown her support behind Vautrin, promising him an alchemist. But she couldn't bring herself to squash the little flicker of hope that Hermine Boucher would see the error of her ways and return to her. She was playing both sides against the middle, confident that whichever faction came out on top, she would triumph with it. Her expression confirmed it was true. And it confirmed she knew Corbeau understood. "Still at the mansion, is he?" Subdued, Sophie nodded again. "You're playing a very dangerous game."

"Like you care."

"How can you—Sophie, you know that's not true."

Shadows flickered across Sophie's face, the candlelight sharpening her features, just as Sophie sharpened her tone. "You don't, you know. You never have."

"That's not true," Corbeau repeated, but guilt and uncertainty had crept into her tone. She had cared once, still did, in a way. But not in the way that Sophie wanted her to. "Anyway, this isn't the time or the place. Innocent people are in danger, and if you have any decency, you'll help me."

"So you haven't come to join us."

"I'm here to do my job. Tell me where they are."

They were there in the building. Sophie's expression made it clear—as clear as her disappointment Corbeau wasn't there to fulfill her fantasies, as clear as the fact Sophie might well thwart Corbeau's efforts just because she could. But the spite left her expression, replaced by a cautious cunning.

"You mean Dr. Kalderash?"

"And three others. Claudine Fournier, the driver Bertrand, and a little boy."

Sophie nodded, narrowing her eyes. Corbeau didn't trust her as far as she could toss her. But Corbeau trusted herself and her knowledge of their past. She trusted her ability to read Sophie's intentions and predict her actions. That, at least, was something.

"They're here."

"Alive?"

"Claudine is here, and Michel Bertrand. Hermine is protecting them. But Armand…"

"Is dead," Corbeau said. "I know. What about—"

"Yes, yes, your precious Dr. Kalderash is here, along with her brat."

"My precious—"

"I know you, Elise. You always need someone to rescue." Sophie laughed cynically. "She's perfect for you. You always did love 'you and me against the world.'"

"You're out of your mind."

But even as she said it, Sophie's words hit a nerve. She'd first felt that nerve when Javert had shown her Kalderash's picture: the intelligent face, the arrogant posture, the simple, tasteful dress. The interview with the inventor had left her livid and convinced of Kalderash's guilt. Still, she'd been forced to admire the woman's brains, her determination in the face of persecution, and her indomitable spirit. And yes, if it came right down to it, Corbeau would have to admit that, despite the mechanical eye and the scars that marred her delicate features—or perhaps because of them—

they were, after all, a physical representation of the inventor's undeniable inner strength—she did find Dr. Kalderash attractive.

But this really was beside the point.

"I have a job to do. Either help me or get out of the way."

"Don't hurt Hermine," Sophie said, vulnerability creeping into her voice. "She's as much a victim as anyone else."

"She's kidnapped a woman, and a child, too."

"You remember what it was like, don't you? Those poor people who came to you to make the voices stop?"

Of course Corbeau remembered. People driven half-mad by bizarre phenomena that occurred all around them. Disembodied voices. Objects moving of their own accord. Fires. Corbeau hadn't understood these phenomena any more than the people who were generating them—not until she'd worked with Vidocq. But she had known how to make them stop. For a price.

And for the additional, unintended price of their health and sanity when Corbeau learned to cut the ingredients in order to maximize her profits.

"Don't you remember how desperate they were? How they'd have done anything to make the demons go away? That's all Hermine wants. I tried, Elise, but I couldn't mix the potions like you could. In the end, I couldn't help, so she wanted Maria back. But Maria refused. So she had to bring her here. Don't you see? You spoke of decency. If you have any at all, when you see her, you'll want to help her as much as I do. You'll be her alchemist. You'll take care of her and help her to minister to all those poor, suffering souls."

And Hermine would be so grateful she'd fly back into Sophie's arms? Not likely. Or perhaps Corbeau would be inspired to pick up their relationship where they'd left off. How far into madness had Madame Hermine Boucher wandered? Would she be able to help her at all, were she so moved? What a mess. If innocent lives weren't at stake, Corbeau would have turned around and left without a second thought. "What about Vautrin?" she asked.

Sophie's lips drew tight. She looked away. "He knows where we are. He'll be here tonight, which is why—"

"And he has most of her followers behind him, I assume." Sophie nodded, looking down. "Sophie...why?"

She looked up, eyes suddenly blazing with fanatic indignation. "We're at war, Elise. An all-out war on demons and the people harboring them. Vautrin and Hermine worked together for a while, but then he got impatient. Said Hermine'd had her chance and failed. Now is the time for force, he said. When he and his followers began to question her openly, she disappeared with the few who were still loyal. Elise, what could I do?" She blinked at Corbeau helplessly, eyes wide, looking as innocent as a porcelain doll in the candlelight.

"You didn't have to tell him where she was, when she would be there, and that she was building the Left Hand of Justice."

"I was angry. After all I'd done for her, she wanted to go back to Maria."

"Out of love, or because she wanted the weapon?"

"Does it matter?"

Corbeau closed her eyes and exhaled. "But now you've changed your mind."

Tears sprang to Sophie's eyes. "I never wanted to hurt Hermine. I thought if Vautrin took over the Divine Spark, she and I could go away quietly and just...be at peace. But Vautrin isn't content to let her just leave. He used her disappearance as a pretext to seize power, and now that she's gone, he wants her gone permanently. He's coming, Elise. Tonight. Help us, please."

Corbeau stared. Hard. Sophie's candle sputtered, drowning in its wax. Corbeau felt much the same way. She shook her head.

"Why did you send me to Vautrin?"

"He's a bad, bad man. He killed Lambert. I knew you would figure it out and punish him."

"You have too much faith in me, Soph."

Sophie put a hand on Corbeau's arm and looked into her eyes. Corbeau sighed. "Can you help us get away? Protect us from Vautrin?"

"Vautrin, whom you led here, right here, at this very moment? Vautrin, who would have loved to see me dead even before all this started—that Vautrin?"

"Hermine brought Maria here to have her build the Left Hand. She doesn't want to use it. She just wants to protect herself. Vautrin has recruited a number of police officers, and he has the ear of the King. If he gets rid of Hermine once and for all, the way will be clear for him to declare war on all those harboring demons. No one will be safe."

"And what about you, Soph? Will you stand by the woman you claim to love, or will you take your place beside the victor, whoever it might be? And if I choose the wrong side, can I expect a knife in my back, too?"

Sophie looked at her miserably, her expression a combination of guilt and helplessness.

"When the time comes, I'm sure you'll do the right thing."

It wasn't the response Corbeau would have hoped for, but it was the one she should have expected. Resisting the impulse to roll her eyes, she gestured toward the hallway in front of her.

"Right. In that case, take me to her."

## CHAPTER FOURTEEN

How much longer?" Hermine snarled. The pistol trembled in her fingers as she paced the length of the small room. It wasn't the gun that Maria feared, though. Between Hermine's lack of experience with the weapon and her current state of derangement, Maria doubted Hermine could hit the side of a house. The real threat, Maria thought, turning a wary eye upward, was the array of tools, glass, and hardware circling above both of their heads in a jerky orbit of spiritual agitation. "Well?"

*Every time you ask me that, it adds an hour to the process,* Maria thought, wishing she had the courage to say it out loud. The debris-cloud shuddered with a metallic clatter, and Maria flinched. All things considered, Hermine was displaying unprecedented restraint, despite her red-ringed eyes and the veins showing blue beneath the pale skin of her face and hands. Her white-blond hair was falling out of the sloppy braid that ran down her thin back. Spiritual energy radiated off her in short, jagged bursts. But Maria knew from experience—bitter experience—that Hermine's frailty was an illusion. As Hermine pinned her with a wild gaze, Maria averted her eyes, focusing again on her work.

What a mistake it had been, telling Hermine about the Left Hand of Justice! She should have seen Hermine's eyes were glowing with avarice, not love. She should have known the device, and not the feelings Hermine had protested—the feelings she still protested—would become her single-minded focus. When Maria had left those months ago, Hermine had sworn the device would be hers. True to her word, she'd bodily dragged Maria back to the lab she'd built for her, to finish it. But Maria was running out of time. Hermine might not know anything about machinery, but she wasn't stupid. Maria could only go on fiddling with wire and screwdrivers for so long before Hermine would realize that Maria had no intention of finishing the weapon.

It was a small comfort that the facilities Hermine had provided were adequate. Somehow Hermine had managed to reproduce the machine lab that Maria had watched her destroy, right down to the jars of washers and screws lined up along the edge of the table. There was an impressive array of tools, as well as metal plates, pins, springs, and cylinders that Maria herself would have ordered for the project. A second table sat at right angles to the first, piled high with canvas, sewing needles, and different thicknesses of cord. Hermine had stood over her while she constructed the canvas sleeve, and there it sat, like the beginnings of a straitjacket, with two rudimentary projectile weapons mounted on the knuckles.

Yes, Maria had been far too trusting at the beginning of their relationship, and she was paying for it now. But at least she could say that even when her feelings had blinded her to Hermine's true intentions, she had possessed the circumspection to withhold the secret of the Left Hand. Without the conductive fabric—that special feather-light weave of metals Maria had sold half of her possessions to commission—the Left Hand of Justice would never be more than an artful combination of metal and cloth.

The basement room had grown stuffy and close. The musty smell of the damp dirt floor tickled the back of her throat. Although Maria knew the air was adequate for herself, Hermine, and little Joseph, who was quietly doing something in the corner involving scraps of metal and wire, Maria felt panic rising in her chest. It was the same kind of crushing, airless, trapped-animal sensation she used to feel when one of Hermine's moods would overtake her. When Hermine would corner her and objects would start flying, Maria had been almost willing to believe in demons.

"Madame, couldn't we keep the door open, just a crack?" Joseph asked, as if sensing Maria's tension. "The doctor—"

"The doctor will finish her work whether the door is open or not," Hermine snapped. She began to pace faster, muttering to herself under her breath. The objects overhead moved faster as well, some of the heavier ones breaking out of their orbit and crashing against the walls.

"Of course I'll finish, Hermine," Maria said. The placating tone of her own voice set her teeth on edge, but she knew better than to agitate the woman further. She eyed a heavy wrench sitting on the table next to the canvas sleeve. "Why don't you try to get some sleep?"

Hermine swung her gun back toward Maria. "Quickly, if you know what's good for you. They'll be here any minute. And keep that brat quiet."

"His name is Joseph, and I'm amazed you can hear anything over the clatter you're making."

A jar of screws suddenly broke away from the floating procession of objects and careened into the wall above Maria's head. Maria instinctively cowered as broken glass and bits of metal rained down. Eyes closed, breath shaking, she waited until it stopped, then straightened and brushed the debris from her hair and dress. She should have known better than to talk back. Hermine had taught her that lesson when Maria had thought they were in love. She slowly opened her eyes and adjusted the barrel of the little gun that would sit above the third finger of the Left Hand. She relaxed a bit when Hermine began to pace again. When the other woman turned, Maria stole another glance at the wrench on the sewing table, imagining its cool weight in her hand.

In another instance of almost supernatural perspicacity, Joseph dropped one of the small pieces of hardware he'd been playing with. Hermine looked over, and Maria pocketed the wrench. Joseph threw her a devilish wink, and Maria nodded her thanks. She'd been lucky that she'd been working when Hermine had come for her. She'd fitted her work dress with several hidden pockets—just like the thick apron that covered them.

Hermine stopped and leaned against the wall, pinching the bridge of her nose between her fingers. Through her fear, Maria felt a pang of sympathy. She'd seen Hermine in any number of bad states, but never like this. "It doesn't have to be this way, you know," Maria said gently. "I could teach you how to control it."

"I don't want to control it. I want it gone."

"I could show you how to turn it into something useful."

"A demon can never be useful."

Maria looked up from the finished projectile weapon now firmly attached to its metal plate. Once she secured it to the canvas sleeve, she would be out of excuses. Hermine would demand a demonstration. She set the piece aside. "It's not a demon, Hermine."

Hermine looked up, eyes flashing. The overhead objects rattled against each other and against the walls. Maria's heart raced, then calmed again as, instead of attacking, Hermine slumped against the wall, her gun hand falling limply to her side. "It's too late for that now. Vautrin has betrayed us. He'll be coming for us tonight, I can feel it. And when he comes, that thing has to be ready. Haven't you figured out what the problem is, at least?"

Maria felt the comforting weight of the wrench in her side pocket. She glanced at Joseph, wondering whether she could drag him to his feet and out the door before Hermine could pull the trigger. "Chief Inspector Vautrin has the entire police department behind him." Well, perhaps not the entire department, Maria thought. If only she'd played it differently with Inspector Corbeau. If only she'd trusted her initial impression of the inspector's honesty and good intent. She thought of the silver medallion she'd tucked into the folds of her shift. Double protection, indeed. She could have used Inspector Corbeau's protection right then. "Instead of waiting for him to come for you, why don't you leave before he gets here?"

It was the wrong thing to say. The thought was impertinent, the suggestion absurd. Maria knew it the second the words left her mouth. The procession of objects above their heads stopped in their orbits, shook, and flung themselves at the wall. As glass and metal rained down all around them, Hermine fixed Maria with a hateful glare and raised the gun.

❖

Corbeau and Sophie stepped off the stairs onto the dirt floor of the basement, greeted with a crash of glass and metal that shook the air. Corbeau put out her arm to keep Sophie back, but Sophie pushed past, instinctively running to a door on the far side of the corridor.

"Hermine!" Sophie pounded on the door with her fist. She shook the doorknob and then ran at the door shoulder-first.

"Stop!" Corbeau grabbed her as she backed up for another run. She held Sophie by the arms, marveling at the fire in the other woman's eyes and the determination thrumming in her small bones. "You'll dislocate your arm. "

"But—"

"And then you'll be no help to Hermine Boucher or anyone else." *Your beloved Hermine*, Corbeau wanted to say, *who kidnapped a woman and a child and is holding them prisoner.* If she was unsure where Sophie's loyalties lay, her desperation to batter down the door clarified things a bit. She placed Sophie against the wall where she could keep an eye on her. "Is that where she's keeping them?" Sophie nodded. "Right. Then stand back. Don't even think about moving until I say so."

Taking a breath, Corbeau raised her knee to her chest and brought her foot down hard on the wood to the left of the doorknob. The wood splintered, and the voices inside came to an abrupt stop. Corbeau lifted her leg and kicked again. The door flew inward and bounced off the wall, where it swung weakly from the mangled hinges. Corbeau stepped back and peered around the doorjamb.

Time and experience had taught her not to rush into an unknown situation, but when she saw Kalderash cowering by the table in a pool of broken glass, a powerful surge of protectiveness threatened to sweep her into the room, caution be damned. This brilliant, compassionate woman had risked her life—who knew how many times?—to continue her healing work. She'd been persecuted by the police and falsely accused of a crime that never happened. Corbeau herself had been ready to arrest her earlier that day. Now that Corbeau knew the truth, she'd be damned if she'd let any further evil befall Maria Kalderash. She might not have been able to save the people that her chemical concoctions had hurt in the past, but here, now, she could at least ensure this. "Sûreté. Is anyone injured?"

"No," Dr. Kalderash said in a tone Corbeau had heard before, from other women afraid an honest answer would result in worse injury once the police had left. Corbeau balled her hands into fists as she watched the inventor slowly straighten, brushing broken glass from her skirt with shaking hands. Kalderash adjusted her hair and cleared her throat. "No one is injured, Inspector."

Corbeau stepped cautiously into the room, Sophie slipping silently in behind her. From behind her came a voice that sent a chill up her spine.

"Very pretty."

Corbeau whirled. "Madame Boucher?"

Sophie swung the door shut. The bent hinges kept it from closing completely, but the meaning of the gesture was clear. A sharp-edged smile broke across Madame Boucher's pale face, sending a shiver of recognition up Corbeau's spine. Hers was a tormented soul. The torment derived not only from the unwanted spiritual energies Corbeau could feel crackling in the air, but also from the inexpertly compounded chemical remedies to which she had subjected herself.

"Did Vautrin send you in first to distract me?"

Madame Boucher wouldn't have looked out of place at Charenton, Corbeau thought as she took in the woman's frantic gaze, disheveled clothes and hair, and the hysteria bubbling at the edges of her voice. The pistol trembling in her hand. Not a few of Corbeau's former customers had found themselves at Charenton. The doctors there were kind but had no understanding of supernatural disturbances.

As Corbeau glanced around at the wreckage strewn across the tables and floor, she felt the low hum of supernatural energy in the air. The jars on the far worktable rattled together. A hammer clattered to the ground.

"I understand," Corbeau said, falling into the calming patter she used to approach a person in the throes of a supernatural outburst. Putting the pistol out of her mind for the moment, she said, "When you're upset, objects move of their own accord." Madame Boucher's eyes enlarged. The suspicion that pinched her features seemed to abate slightly. Encouraged, Corbeau said, "You can control it, you know. It's in your power to make it stop."

"Demons."

Corbeau shook her head. One eye on the pistol, the other on Sophie, she circled around slowly, stopping before Maria Kalderash, who relaxed as Corbeau positioned herself between her and the gun. Corbeau felt an unexpected satisfaction; at least she could provide the inventor this small protection. A flash of motion in the corner of her eye told her that Joseph was nearby. Willing him to stay where he was, she put her hand into her bag and felt for her bottle of pills. "You can control these outbursts with training. But right now—"

"Liar!" Corbeau jerked her hand away from the bag. "You're an agent of the Sûreté. You're just trying to keep me busy until Vautrin gets here."

"Believe me, Gustave Vautrin is no friend of mine," Corbeau said. She smiled encouragingly, but the spell was broken. Madame Boucher had brought her other hand up to steady the pistol, which meant if she pulled the trigger now, she might actually be able to hit someone.

"She's an alchemist," Sophie suddenly said. Hermine glanced over, and Sophie stepped toward her. Hermine flinched as Sophie laid her hands on her shoulders, then relaxed slightly. Corbeau felt some of her own tension depart—until she remembered that Sophie would betray them all the minute Vautrin arrived. Or would she? "A real alchemist," Sophie said. "Not like me. She can help. Please let her help, Hermine."

Corbeau narrowed her eyes. Sophie had sent her to Vautrin, not to the building where she and Hermine were hiding from Vautrin. She loved Hermine Boucher but was feathering a nest on Vautrin's side, just in case events shook out in his favor. Madame Boucher swallowed. She glanced from Sophie to Corbeau and back again. She had less reason to trust Sophie than Corbeau did. But they could sort that out after the pistol was out of the equation.

"Lay your weapon on the table," Corbeau said. Looking closer at the pistol, she saw that it was an old blunderbuss—the kind that shot a single lead ball. It had probably last seen action before any of them were born and had most likely been hanging on someone's wall since then. Was it even loaded? But one look at Madame Boucher's face, the white knuckles barely restraining themselves against the trigger, made Corbeau unwilling to take the risk. "Put the weapon down, or—"

A sudden impact shook the house. Corbeau and Sophie exchanged a look. The crash came again, this time so hard that it shook the floorboards above them.

"Back door," Corbeau said. "Vautrin?" Sophie nodded.

Hermine glanced from Kalderash to Corbeau, as if trying to evaluate which was the greater threat. Then she trained the pistol on Corbeau. Corbeau stepped backward, hands raised. She felt the warm solidity of Maria Kalderash at her back, felt her heart pounding through her simple dark dress. She reached backward and found the inventor's hand, whose fingers closed around hers. Her hands were surprisingly steady, and Corbeau was surprised that her touch conveyed as much comfort as Corbeau had hoped the doctor would receive from the gesture.

What was not a pleasant surprise was the realization that crept over Sophie's face, and the steel in her eyes as she took in their locked fingers. Corbeau was very grateful Sophie wasn't holding the pistol. She took another step back and realized Dr. Kalderash was now trapped between her and a table. She gave the inventor's fingers a squeeze and stepped to one side, keeping herself in the path of the gun.

Footsteps clattered up the stairs to the second floor. Vautrin's men were checking the upstairs rooms first. Corbeau glanced upward at the sound of slamming doors and surprised cries. Bertrand and Fournier, from what Sophie had said. The women glanced at each other, from one to the next, as the sounds of struggle moved along the second floor hallway, back down the stairs.

"They're coming," Hermine whispered. Corbeau held her breath as Hermine's eyes tracked the path of the footsteps.

Dr. Kalderash sprang past Corbeau, pulling a heavy wrench from the folds of her dress. Corbeau stepped out to stop her, but Kalderash pushed her aside with astounding speed and swung the wrench down on Madame Boucher's gun-arm with all her strength. Metal met skin with a sickening crack.

There was a flash and a roar. Some unstoppable, invisible force propelled Corbeau back into a workbench. Pain radiated out from her left shoulder, enveloping her in a numb wave. She watched as Sophie ran to Hermine's side, and Kalderash, clearly horrified, watched Corbeau slide to the floor.

The blunderbuss had been loaded, then, Corbeau thought. And the pistol had been fully functional. Sticky warmth spilled over her breasts. Breathing was agony. She couldn't feel her left arm.

"Inspector!" Kalderash cried.

Corbeau fought back the fog gathering at the periphery of her vision. She concentrated on the shards of glass poking through her borrowed trousers. She rolled a metal screw between her fingers, marveling at its coolness. Swallowing, she forced herself to speak. "I know about the Left Hand of Justice…about…the Department of…of the Unexplained."

"Don't speak." Kalderash knelt beside her, nudging the pistol beneath the table. She unbuttoned Corbeau's coat.

"I know you've committed no crime, and that…that…you're here against your will."

"Be quiet." Corbeau tried to help Kalderash get her out of the coat, but every time she moved, the pain threatened to swallow her. Yet the pain was the only thing standing between her and oblivion. She clung to it like a drowning man. "We have to stop the bleeding." Kalderash brought her face to Corbeau's. There was no sound, save for the clicking and whirring of the mechanical eye. "It's going to hurt."

Corbeau looked into the depths of the inventor's natural eye. She nodded. "Do it."

Kalderash glanced over her shoulder, to where Hermine, whimpering, was cradling her ruined arm in her lap.

"You broke her wrist," Sophie said.

"Splint it." Kalderash nodded toward the assortment of canvas and metal on the worktable.

Corbeau's left arm was free, the coat hanging loose from her right. Dr. Kalderash ripped open the front of her blouse. As Kalderash bound her wound, Corbeau watched Sophie fashion a competent splint. She had been a good assistant, Corbeau remembered. A fast learner. As if sensing Corbeau's thoughts, Sophie glanced over at her. Madame Boucher's wrist was swelling, the hand at an unnatural angle. But the splint was sound. Excruciating pain called her back to the situation at hand.

"Sorry," Kalderash said.

Corbeau's upper arm looked like ground meat. There was so much blood it was impossible to tell where it was coming from. Everything hurt.

Kalderash bound her shoulder with canvas. "Have to stop the bleeding, stabilize the arm. I'm not going to try to take the bullet out now. We have to get out of here before Vautrin finds us. Are you able to stand?"

Corbeau's legs shook as Kalderash helped her slowly to her feet. The room swayed for a moment. Corbeau leaned against a table. "I was supposed to be helping you." Her voice came out a painful gasp. Kalderash looked at her quizzically, a smile playing at the edge of her lips.

"I do appreciate it, Inspector." Kalderash paused for a moment, then produced a small metal disk from somewhere in the folds of her clothing and pressed it into Corbeau's good hand. "I believe this belongs to you, now." The disk was cool against her palm. It was etched with designs that swam before her eyes as she tried, futilely, to focus on them. Kalderash closed Corbeau's fingers around the disk and slipped her hand into her pocket. "I'll explain later," she said.

Corbeau's entire left side throbbed. Her mind went to the sedatives in her waist bag. They would certainly take the edge off, but they would also render her useless—not that she was much use as it was. Footsteps shuffling across the floor above them reminded her that Vautrin and his men were still in the building. Raised voices. Someone moving furniture. They were probably securing Bertrand and Fournier so they'd have their hands free when they came down to the basement.

"Make a barricade," Corbeau heard Kalderash tell Sophie. But her voice sounded far away. The room swayed. Corbeau faltered, catching herself on the table at the last moment. In an instant, Kalderash was at her side. When Kalderash looked at her shoulder, she paled. "There's too much blood," she said. "I'll have to redo the dressing."

"No time," Sophie said as footsteps rang in the staircase once more. "They're here."

## CHAPTER FIFTEEN

"Make a barricade," Maria said. Glancing at Hermine, Sophie jumped up to obey. Joseph, stuffing his bits and bobs in his pocket, scrambled to help her clear the canvas scraps from a table and push it across the doorway. "No good. Turn it on its side and put whatever you can behind it. Wedge a chair beneath the knob."

"It won't work. The door was compromised when I kicked it in."

Maria looked down at the inspector, hoping her fear didn't show on her face. She'd done the best she could with the wound, but there was so much blood, pooling around her legs and soaking into the packed earth of the basement floor. The bullet was lodged in Corbeau's shattered shoulder. The wound was ugly, and the inspector was sweating and pale.

"Be still," Maria said as Corbeau clumsily felt around her coat pocket. Ignoring her, the inspector pulled out Armand's medallion, running a finger over the etched design. *Double protection.* Inspector Corbeau had come to protect her, had put herself between Maria and Hermine's gun. Now Maria was protecting her from her injuries—and from Vautrin, if she had anything to say about it. Not double protection, then, but mutual protection. She cocked her head. It had been a long time since she'd been in a situation that was even remotely mutual.

"Finished," Sophie said, interrupting her thoughts.

Maria inspected the new barricade. Sophie had jammed the edge of a table underneath the doorknob and piled the remaining furniture behind the table. The door was in bad shape, as the inspector had said. But all things considered, Sophie had done a good job. She also appeared to have made an excellent splint out of the admittedly meager available materials. "I'm impressed," she told Sophie. "Do you have medical training?"

Sophie looked away. "I used to help Elise when…well…that was a long time ago."

Corbeau and Sophie glanced at one another. Maria felt something pass between them and was surprised that she felt a little jealous. But she didn't have time to entertain emotional fancies. She wished Corbeau were more mobile. She'd have been good in a battle.

"There's no way we're going to simply walk out of here, is there?" Sophie asked.

Maria shook her head. It was only a matter of time before Vautrin found them. Even if the barricade held, they would just wait them out. Maria glanced over at Hermine. She had stopped whimpering, but she was cradling her arm and staring at the wall, her mind somewhere very far away. At one time, Maria might have felt her pain, or at least felt remorse for having caused it. But that time was long past.

"Where's the gun?" Corbeau rasped.

Maria almost answered, but something in Corbeau's voice told her that if she did, Corbeau would dive under the table to retrieve it. Maria glanced under the table, but she didn't see anything. Perhaps she'd kicked it harder than she'd thought.

"You find somewhere safe to sit this out. You're not fighting anyone with that arm."

"I've seen worse," Corbeau countered.

"You certainly will if you don't do as I say." She caught Sophie's eye and gestured toward Hermine. "Put her in the corner behind the table. You too, Inspector."

A door slammed overhead. Footsteps sounded on the basement stairs. Several sets of feet thundered down toward the basement, wood splintering beneath their weight. Another crash sounded above.

"Hurry!" Maria cried.

Maria helped Corbeau away from the machine table and propped her against a wall. Then she and Sophie swept everything off the table, tipped it over, and moved Hermine behind it. Joseph, Maria noted with irritation, had run to Corbeau's side. She was leaning down close, and he was speaking excitedly into her ear. The gun was nowhere to be seen.

"I really wish the two of you would get behind the table."

"While you fight them off all alone?"

Maria gaped at Joseph's temerity, but the sudden silence drowned her objections. Even worse than the silence was the subsequent, and most incongruently, polite knock on the door.

"Madame Boucher?" Maria recognized the chief inspector's voice. His tone was solicitous. Mocking. "I know you're in there, Madame. Why don't you come out?"

Maria glanced at Hermine, who had begun to tremble— though whether it was from her injuries or from imagining what Vautrin would enjoy doing to her once he found her, Maria wasn't sure. Maria's gut clenched at the sound of the masculine laughter that followed. She counted four distinct voices. She and Sophie were two—with Joseph, perhaps two and a half. It was futile. But she'd escaped futile circumstances before.

"Arm yourself," she told Sophie. Hermine's lover had shown unexpected medical skills. Perhaps she'd be better in a fight than she looked. "Grab anything. Anything. Fight like hell and run when you can."

"What about them?" Sophie asked, gesturing toward Hermine.

"Come out, come out, wherever you are."

Maria nodded, and Sophie positioned herself next to the doorjamb, an iron bar in her hand.

The door gave way beneath the first kick. The second sent the table and chairs crashing backward.

"Now!" Maria cried as the first man pushed his way through the crack.

But Sophie stepped back, letting the bar drop to her side. "Great Prophet," she said, bowing her head as Vautrin entered.

The betrayal hit Maria like a punch. She stared, speechless, as the chief inspector stepped over the wreckage, surveying the room like a conqueror. He glanced at Sophie, then, apparently satisfied, gestured her to the side with his pistol. Maria held her breath as his eyes passed over her, noting her presence as if she were another object in a newly acquired inventory. When he spoke, his tone held a note of disappointment.

"We meet again, Doctor. How I wish I had the time to finish what I started when you first came to our fair city." He shrugged. "Ah, well, as the English say, 'if A's and An's were pots and pans—'"

Maria's heart stopped when Vautrin's foul gaze landed on the inspector. Corbeau met his eyes and held them. The mutual animosity passing between them was palpable in the close atmosphere of the basement room. A sharp smile played around the chief inspector's mouth. Maria balled her hands into fists as he chuckled beneath his breath, no doubt planning how he would dispose of Corbeau. Vautrin turned back to Sophie.

"Where is she? Where is the original Prophet?"

Maria's fingers itched for the wrench in her pocket. But while Vautrin had been assessing the situation, three of his men had trickled into the room behind him. Two, like Vautrin, were armed. The third was carrying a metal container with a pump and nozzle, looking around the room with purpose. Not wanting to attract attention to the only weapon she was likely to get, Maria wiped her palms on her skirt, taking comfort from the cool metal concealed within its folds.

Then, slowly, incrementally, the air began to vibrate around them. The vibrations grew stronger, thrumming against Maria's skin. The jars, broken glass, and bits of metal on the workbench began to rattle in sympathy. Vautrin looked panicked at first. Then, when Hermine gave a choked gasp, he turned to her, an unpleasant mixture of triumph and cruelty creeping over his face. "Well, Inspector," he said, turning back to Corbeau. "I see you've found your missing heiress. And her kidnapper, too. Won't your master Javert be proud of you?"

Heat rushed to Maria's face. She felt another stab of betrayal, and inexplicable disappointment. Corbeau had been working for Javert all along. She had said she knew Maria had committed no crime, but Sophie had betrayed Hermine so easily. Would Corbeau betray her to Javert, if they managed to escape Vautrin?

"It's too bad your honors will all be posthumous." The man with the metal canister pointed the nozzle at a pile of rags and gave the pump-handle a push. The smell of kerosene cut through the air, acrid and sharp. Maria clutched the wrench through the fabric of her dress as the man continued around the room, dousing wood and fabric in the flammable oil. "The newspapers will tell of an unfortunate fire that took three lives: the tragic Madame Boucher, her villainous Gypsy captor, and the brave Sûreté agent who tried to save her. Are you getting this, Mademoiselle Martin? The story will be yours, exclusively."

"Yes, Great Prophet."

Maria looked over at the inspector. Corbeau looked pained, and not just from her injury. She felt Sophie's betrayal as keenly as any of them. Hermine stirred in the corner. When she spoke, her voice was a disbelieving moan.

"Why?"

Vautrin's man rewarded her with a splash of oil. Maria winced as Hermine sputtered and swiped at her face with her one good hand. Where was Joseph, Maria suddenly wondered. She didn't dare hope he had escaped the building, but at least he'd escaped Vautrin's attention. She allowed a brief spark of hope to dance in her mind, while she let her fingers dance over the wrench in her pocket.

❖

"It's to your master Javert that we all owe this fortuitous meeting. Go upstairs and watch the others," he said to the man blocking the door. "This won't take long." He returned his attention to Madame Boucher. As he spoke, he gestured expansively with the pistol. "The prefect told me your organization was developing some weapon. That didn't interest me, at least not at first. I saw opportunity—an opportunity that had eluded me to that point. I realize now that before then, the time simply wasn't right. I had been trying to make things happen, when I should have been waiting for them to fall into place.

"When I heard Madame Boucher speak, I knew that the Lord was finally—*finally*—giving me the chance to fulfill the Church's highest calling."

"Caring for the vulnerable?" Corbeau asked. Speaking hurt. Vautrin regarded her with hatred, but then smiled maliciously.

"No, Inspector. Rooting out demons and the sinners who harbor them." He turned to Madame Boucher. "At first I really did think you were a prophet. The way you spoke. Such passion. Such clarity of vision. You moved people. But you were weak. It was only a matter of time before your own demons overtook you. The others saw it too—at least after I pointed it out."

"That wasn't the goal," Hermine said. "The goal was to help people—"

"Same thing, different words. You had your chance to do it your way, and you failed. Now your followers are my followers, and together, with the might of the King, the Church, and the police behind us, we'll finish what the Inquisition started. But first." His head swiveled toward Dr. Kalderash. Despite the heat that radiated from her wound, the gesture made Corbeau's blood run cold. She wanted to jump up, to kick that vile expression off his face, or at least to put herself between them. "Where is the Left Hand of Justice?"

"It's not here."

"Liar." He raised the pistol. "I know she brought you here to finish it."

Kalderash's mechanical Eye clicked and whirred—probably, Corbeau thought, as she scrambled for a plausible deception. Vautrin knew Hermine had brought the inventor there to work on the Arm. But he didn't know Corbeau had the gossamer sheet of woven metal in her bag. Corbeau still wasn't certain what the mesh did. But it was the secret—of this she was sure. Without it, the Left Hand of Justice wouldn't function.

"What would you do with it?" Corbeau asked. Had to keep him talking while she figured out what to do. But what could she do, really? Just speaking shot waves of pain through her body. Kalderash had bound her shoulder so tightly her fingers had gone numb. Her knees trembled, but Vautrin didn't seem to notice.

"Unfortunately, you won't be around to witness that. Oh, it would have been sweet to finish you off with my bare hands." He shrugged regretfully. "If only there were time." He turned the gun back on Kalderash. The man with the kerosene canister mumbled under his breath. He must have finished his task. The fumes were thick in the stale basement air. Corbeau's eyes and throat burned. Vautrin gave a sharp nod. "Gentlemen?"

Taking their cue, the other two men began to move toward the door. Vautrin tucked the pistol into his waistband, then reached into his coat pocket. As he brought out his tinderbox, he met Corbeau's eyes.

"Such a shame you weren't ultimately able to save the heiress, Inspector. You made a valiant attempt. But the fire consumed her so suddenly."

He raised his hand to strike the flint. Then there came a sick, wet crunch. For a moment, Vautrin hung in the air, a surprised expression on his face. He crumpled to the ground, dark blood pooling around his shattered skull.

Sophie stood behind him, the metal bar in her hand. For a moment, she blinked at Corbeau, as if she had no idea how she'd found herself there. "I couldn't let him hurt Hermine." She turned to Madame Boucher. "Even if…even if you don't want me anymore…I just couldn't…"

Corbeau nodded, but Sophie wasn't looking at her anymore. Corbeau watched as she went to Hermine's side. A movement caught her eye.

"Soph!"

One of Vautrin's men had found his way back inside. Seeing Vautrin, he swung his canister down toward Sophie's head. Suddenly Joseph sprang from beneath a pile of canvas, flinging Corbeau's phial of iron filings into the man's face—just as she'd told him to. Then he flung a handful of screws and nuts onto the floor in his path. The man dropped the canister and fell to the ground, clawing at his eyes. Sophie rolled away, shielding Hermine with her body.

"Where's the other—" The words died in Corbeau's throat as she saw the third man go for the tinderbox. Instinctively, she lunged toward him—a costly mistake. Her legs buckled beneath her and she pitched forward. As she hit the floor—the impact practically blinding her with pain—something rough brushed against her face. Dr. Kalderash streaked across the room—where had she been standing?—and brought the man down with one swift blow from her wrench. "Where'd you get that?"

Kalderash looked down at Corbeau with a mixture of self-consciousness and pride, and shrugged. "I've been in this situation before. More often than you'd care to know."

The pain in her arm had gone from an explosive burn to a heavy numbness that wrapped her body and squeezed the breath from her chest. Gasping, Corbeau rested her cheek against the dirt floor. The dizzying smells of kerosene, packed earth, and blood filled her nostrils. Her pulse pounded in her ears. A scuffle caught her attention, and she turned her head. Through the spots dancing in front of her eyes, she made out a figure in the doorway.

"Inspector!" Javert sounded entirely too cheerful for the situation he was stepping into—or the prone bodies he was stepping over. "Lying down on the job? Well, it seems you have the situation under control, at any rate." Corbeau groaned. "Come on, then, pick yourself up. We've got a long night ahead of us if we're going to come up with a report that explains all this."

❖

"You could have shown up sooner," Corbeau mumbled, as two of Javert's strapping men carried her out on a stretcher toward his waiting fiacre. For the first time in months, the stars were poking holes through the black cloth of the sky. The situation was a tangled mess, but she had no doubt Javert would weave a tidy story and deliver it on a silver platter to His Majesty before the doctors had even finished stitching her up.

"And rob you of the case that will make your career?" Javert smiled. "Does it hurt as much as it looks?"

Corbeau made a noncommittal noise. Joseph had quietly slipped her a few tablets from her bag. They hadn't done much to dull the pain, but they had made her care less about it. The cold night air was bracing.

"You're lucky Vautrin picked tonight to betray Madame Boucher, or we wouldn't have known to come at all."

Through the gauzy veil of pain and drugs, she watched others attend to Madame Boucher and Sophie.

"Madame is injured."

"It's a broken arm, Inspector. She'll mend."

Physically, probably. But then what? Sophie would land on her feet. She always did. But Madame? Would she rebuild her organization and continue her work in the slums? Would she return to her well-appointed house and retire behind the curtains of privilege? Would she and Sophie come back together, their union made stronger by having survived this ordeal? Or would she remember how Sophie had betrayed her at the last moment? Corbeau hoped it would be the former, for both of their sakes, but she'd seen too much in her life to put a lot of stock in hope.

They stopped to watch as Javert's men helped Madame Boucher to a police carriage. Javert's own stood behind it in its unblemished splendor. As the men bearing her lifted her on the count of three, Corbeau asked, "What about—"

"Mademoiselle Fournier and Monsieur Bertrand?" He gestured with his chin toward where they were standing, speaking to a pair of officers that Corbeau vaguely recognized. "Unharmed. Apparently Madame Boucher was hiding them from Vautrin. He's dead, by the way. Any idea how that happened?"

"None." Corbeau closed her eyes. The cold November wind blew across her face. She shivered, but the wind felt good against her hot, hot skin. Ugly Jacques would be off her back and probably more kindly disposed, should she need his services in the future. She hoped she wouldn't. "But what about Dr. Kalderash?"

"Dr. Kalderash?" Javert said, as if he'd never heard the name before. He made an exaggerated frown and rubbed his chin. "Was she there?"

Corbeau cracked an eye open. "You didn't see her?"

Javert turned his frown to her. She searched his face, but the mask was as impenetrable as ever. "I'm not saying that she wasn't there, Inspector. I'm saying that I didn't see her. When I came in, the only thing I could see was that you had rescued Madame Boucher and several others, at great cost to yourself. There will definitely be a commendation in it for you. But as for Dr. Kalderash…" He shrugged.

Corbeau closed her eyes and exhaled heavily. He refused to elaborate, but his answer would have to do for now. Javert had been standing in the doorway. There was no way he could have failed to see Dr. Kalderash, and no way she could have escaped without his knowledge.

He had let her go.

Javert's men slid her inside the carriage, onto the floor, which had been thoughtfully laid with a blanket. It was scratchy and thin, and she could feel the floorboards through it, but she was grateful for the thought nonetheless.

"One last thing, Inspector," Javert said. He was looking down from the doorway of the carriage, his face upside down above Corbeau's. "I don't suppose you found a working prototype?"

"No."

He regarded her for a moment, as if trying to decide whether to probe further. Then he smiled. "I didn't think so. My men searched her rooms thoroughly but didn't uncover either the plans or the conductive fabric. Yes, conductive," he responded before she could ask the question. "The metal forms an interface between the device's trigger mechanisms and the wearer's spiritual energy field—the same energy that, in high concentration, causes such trouble for people like poor Madame Boucher. The Left Hand of Justice would have been the first weapon controlled entirely by the wearer's intention. Pity. Perhaps we can discuss it further when you're feeling more yourself."

*I knew it,* Corbeau thought. She laughed weakly. Javert's frown deepened.

"With all due respect, Monsieur," she heard Joseph say from his dark corner of the carriage, "I think the inspector's been through enough for today."

Javert turned his scowl toward the boy. But then he nodded. "I agree. We'll discuss this later, Inspector. Driver, to the Hôtel-Dieu."

The door clicked carefully shut above her head. She heard the prefect's boots step backward on the uneven pavement. She would really have to have a look at the canvas sleeve Dr. Kalderash had used to bind her shoulder. She looked forward to testing the very functional-looking mechanisms attached to it with the gossamer woven metal in her shoulder bag. Corbeau laughed again, but the pills had rendered the sound fuzzy and weak. Joseph looked down with concern. Corbeau winked.

Above them, the driver snapped his whip above the horses' heads. With a lurch, the carriage began to roll.

## EPILOGUE

By February, Paris had begun to stir beneath its thick, gray blankets of snow and cloud. The wind had lost its bite, and a festive feeling was in the air, as the entire city looked forward to the approach of spring.

It had been a long winter for Corbeau. Recovery had been arduous, painful, and incomplete. But halfway between the bitter end of January and the first rays of the March sun, her day of decision arrived. Wrapping herself tightly in her coat and scarf, she locked her apartment tight, scraped together a few sous, and indulged in a cab ride to the Conciergerie.

The building looked as imposing as ever beneath its cover of snow—snow now hard from melting and refreezing over the course of each day, rather than soft, fresh fall. Icicles hung at intervals along the roof, their sides diminished, slick, and dripping in the midmorning sun. As she approached the entrance, she walked gingerly. The packed snow had melted the day before, and the pavement was treacherous with ice.

"Inspector!" Laveau called as he recognized her. He seemed happy to see her, and relieved. His face fell, though, when he registered her careful gait and her arm still bound to her side rather than filling the left sleeve of her coat. "Not quite back in fighting form yet?"

"It'll take time. You heard what happened."

"All of Paris heard what happened. A lot of people think you're dead."

"Only my enemies, I hope. How's the family?"

He shrugged his broad shoulders. "Fed. Housed. Still, I'd give my firstborn to be back chasing ghosts. Not that I'm complaining," he added, glancing around warily. "Listen, Inspector, I'd invite you inside where it's warm, but we're on tight security after—"

"It's all right, Laveau." Prefect Javert materialized beside the young man. He must have caught sight of her through a window and come outside to meet her, though she hadn't heard or seen his approach. He wasn't wearing a coat, and as fine as his jacket was, it was no match for the chill. He blew on his hands and rubbed them together. "Inspector, I've been expecting you for some weeks, now. Won't you come inside?"

"Thank you."

She followed Javert through the arched entryway. This time the guard didn't even look up from his scandal sheet when she passed by. They continued into the interior of the building, their boot-steps echoing off the stone walls and high, buttressed ceilings, winding through a series of ever-narrower passages until Corbeau wouldn't have been able to find her way out without a trail of bread crumbs. At last they came to a small door at the end of a long, dim hallway. Javert took out a key and unlocked the door.

His office at the Conciergerie looked much the same as the one at his home, minus the statues and expensive wine. It was tidy. Priestly. The walls not lined with bookshelves were papered with mounted maps annotated in his neat hand and stuck with pins and ribbons. The furniture was plain but well made. A small Persian carpet lay beneath the desk and chairs, the only visible concession to comfort. Corbeau doubted his Majesty had issued the rug.

"Welcome back, Inspector. Please sit."

Corbeau glanced at the dark wood chair. "I'll stand. This won't take long."

"As you wish." He took his own chair—wide, padded, with arms—behind the desk and leaned forward, balancing his chin on steepled fingers. "I don't suppose that, in the course of your vacation, you turned up the plans that woman stole from me?"

"No," Corbeau said, though she was wearing the canvas sleeve beneath her shirt. After a thorough cleaning, it had made an excellent support for her arm. She had also begun to make progress with the conductive fabric, though the most she had coaxed from it were a few sparks.

"You haven't seen her?" Javert's tone told her that he knew she'd looked. She and Joseph had scoured the streets as best as they could, but Kalderash had disappeared. Her house was empty and locked up tight. The prefect's perspicacity might have been uncomfortable, had she not decided to leave police work altogether.

"Not since that night. Sir, the reason I came," she fumbled the buckles of her shoulder bag open with her good hand and removed an envelope, "was to tender my resignation." She pushed the envelope across the desk at him. He glanced from the envelope to her, his thick eyebrows knitting together across the bridge of his nose. "I apologize in advance for the handwriting. As you probably know, I'm left-handed."

"Resignation? Surely not? Not now, when we need you, Inspector—or, should I say, Chief Inspector—more than ever before?"

"Chief..."

Corbeau sank down onto the hard chair. She'd anticipated he'd offer her job back, possibly even with more pay. But though it was what she'd wanted more than anything several months ago, she couldn't go back to work on Javert's terms. He had manipulated her. He had invented a crime to entrap an innocent person—a person, she realized too late, she had cared about. If she allowed him to reinstate her in her current position, she would be naming a price for her professional integrity. She would be inviting him to do it again. But as chief inspector...

"With Vautrin gone, there's no one better suited for the position." Leaving her envelope where it was, he slid a stack of papers across the desk to her. Duties, responsibilities, and a contract. "Your first assignment will be to re-staff the Sûreté with qualified agents. After that, I'll expect you to rebuild the Bureau of Supernatural Investigations as quickly as you can.

"And there will be a significant increase in your pay," he added when she still said nothing. "As well as that of your subordinates. It was shameful what they were expecting you to live on." He laid a leather envelope on top of the paper stack. Beneath the unsealed flap, she could see that the envelope was heavy with coin. "An advance," he said, "nothing more."

Corbeau's heart pounded. During those long, cold weeks of recovery, she'd made a plan. After resigning, she'd move into one of the spare rooms at Madame Bernard's house in the Montagne Ste. Geneviève and start compounding again—not sloppy formulae produced for a quick profit, but some of the recipes she'd learned in her childhood. Healing recipes. With Dr. Kalderash gone, the Montagne Ste. Geneviève would need someone to brew medicines, and she, at least, had some knowledge. It would be a difficult life, but not impossible. As a life of service often was.

But as chief inspector, she would have a budget and staff. And she'd be serving not just the people of the Montagne Ste. Geneviève, but all of Paris. What's more, she'd have the authority to do it her way.

"My department," she ventured, "to be run without your interference, the way I see fit?"

Javert cocked an eyebrow. "I wouldn't have it any other way. And I know you wouldn't, either."

"What about the King? What would he say about reinstating the Bureau?"

Javert laughed. "Oh, we mustn't ever tell him. But he won't dare come poking around. I was his confessor, once."

He slid her resignation back toward her. She let it lie. Unlike the King, she didn't trust Javert. She would never trust him completely.

On the other hand, it didn't mean they couldn't work together.

"I'll think about it," she said.

"You'll think about it? Inspector, do you know how many people would jump at the—"

"I'll think about it," Corbeau repeated. "And you'll wait for my response. You'll put in a temporary chief, if you must, but you will wait. You need me." She tucked the money and the contracts into her bag and stood.

Javert continued to stare. Then a slow smile spread over his face. He held up his hands and shrugged. "Of course, Madame. I shall await your pleasure."

He stood to see her out. She slipped her resignation off his desk and crumpled it into her pocket. An unaccustomed elation settled over her: relief, optimism, and the knowledge she'd made the right decision. Nodding once at the prefect, she turned to leave, a small smile pulling at the edges of her lips.

Corbeau stepped out into the brisk, clean, early afternoon. All along the wide Boulevard du Palais, smartly dressed people moved from shop to restaurant to café, weaving in and out between bare trees and piles of dirt-speckled, hardened snow. She considered the question of lunch. The lump of cash in her bag would allow her to eat her meals wherever she pleased for a long time to come. She could travel by cab all over the city for months. Or, she could husband the money carefully and not have to deal with Javert again until the summer.

She decided to enjoy the walk.

What had become of Dr. Maria Kalderash? Corbeau supposed it was inevitable that the inventor would disappear again. Javert might have let her go that long-ago night in November, but he still thought she had the plans for the Left Hand of Justice. If she remained in Paris, he wouldn't have been able to leave her alone for long. And there was Madame Boucher. The headlines had blazed with the names of Hermine Boucher and the Church of the Divine Spark through most of December. But both vanished from the papers some time around the New Year. And now, it was as if neither had ever existed. Even if Madame Boucher and Dr. Kalderash had come to an understanding, could either of them have remained in Paris, under the weight of those memories?

She strode down the boulevard. The day was fine, and she was feeling strong. A flash of red down on the corner caught her eye.

"Sophie!" she called.

The other woman turned. A smile broke over her face and she waved. "Elise!"

They hadn't seen one another since that night in November. Corbeau hadn't pursued her, and Sophie hadn't sought her out. Corbeau was surprised at how happy she was to see Sophie running toward her, her crimson redingote peeking out from beneath her new coat, fur hat bobbing up and down as she ran, her shiny boots clacking on the pavement. As she approached, Corbeau reached out her hand. Sophie took it but stopped short of a full embrace.

"I trust you've been well, Elise," she said soberly.

Corbeau nodded. "You?" Sophie nodded back. She was afraid, Corbeau realized—and rightfully so—that Corbeau wouldn't forgive her for her betrayal in November. And Corbeau hadn't, not for a long time. But those months of solitude and recovery had given her a lot to think about. And although they would never again share the intimacy they once had, Corbeau had too few friends who knew her from the inside out to cut her off completely. "And Madame Boucher?"

Sophie's smile returned. She looked both contented and relieved. "She forgave me, Elise, after I convinced her that I'd seen the error of my ways."

"Have you?"

Sophie looked down. "I think so."

"Is she still having her outbursts?"

Sophie nodded. "It was a little rough after the whole business in November, but we left Paris for a while to rest and heal. She has a small cottage in the country, so quiet and clean. It's doing us a lot of good."

Corbeau shook her head. She couldn't imagine Sophie voluntarily exiling herself from the nonstop excitement of the city, from her luxurious apartment and many lovers. But she looked healthy, happy even. Perhaps the move was just what she needed. "I'm glad. So what are you doing back here?"

Sophie laughed. "Looking for you, of all things. You've been very hard to find."

"Sorry. Jacques gave me good practice."

Sophie made a dismissive gesture. "No matter. I knew if you weren't at home, I could probably find you here. I have some information you might want."

"No more supernatural emergencies, I hope. I'm on vacation."

"Well…"

"Out with it, Soph."

Sophie patted her hair and made a little moue. "All right. I have it on good authority that a small village near Provins has been experiencing strange events. Bangs and crashes in the night, odd-colored flashes of lightning in clear weather, that sort of thing."

"I said I'm on vacation."

"They say it all began with the arrival of a doctor from Paris. She arrived from Paris, that is, but everyone's certain that she's really from somewhere else. They say she's unnaturally talented with machines, and even wears a mechanical eye."

Corbeau's heart stopped. She'd thought quite a bit about Dr. Kalderash in the past few weeks, and not only because she'd been playing with the woman's equipment. She'd never met anyone like her, and she was pretty sure she never would again. Excitement rose in her chest, and, to her surprise, she found herself returning Sophie's smile. "That's good information, Soph."

"I thought you could use it, Inspector."

"That's Chief Inspector, now. And thanks."

Sophie reached up and kissed her on the cheek. It was a chaste kiss, like that of a sister…or a friend. Corbeau opened her mouth to speak, but Sophie was already dancing away in the opposite direction, the bloodred hem of her redingote darting out from beneath her coat, as ever out of reach of the mud and slush. Corbeau watched her disappear into the crowd as light, clean snow began to fall.

❖

Corbeau reached the walled city of Provins in late April. She had left a few weeks after she'd talked to Sophie, making her way slowly, east by southeast, a bit more than one hundred kilometers. The weather had been cooperative; she'd made most of the journey on foot, sleeping under the stars and stopping at the occasional inn as the mood took her. The advance on her salary had lasted well. If she was careful, she'd have enough to return.

She passed through the narrow, twisting cobblestone streets and closely packed houses. Everywhere, the famous Provins roses were exploding into bloom. The air was heavy with their perfume. She wandered for a while through a bustling market and bought a jar of rose honey. She stopped at a tavern for a proper meal and then continued on toward the city gate.

The afternoon sun warmed her shoulders and back. The snow was long gone, and the rolling hills were springing to life in all their green glory. She walked along the path for a few hours more until she came to a small farming settlement. Large parcels of land sprawled out along the hills, with occasional houses dotting the hills here and there. So different from Paris. It looked happy and alive. Even the mud in the wheel-ruts looked clean.

She stepped off the road when she heard the heavy *clip-clop* of a draft horse behind her, followed by the low rumble of its cart.

"Can I help you?" the driver asked, pulling to a stop next to her. He was a pleasant-looking man of about sixty, and he spoke in an easy, country drawl.

"I'm looking for the new doctor, Dr. Kalderash."

Her clipped Parisian sounded harsh in her ears. The man squinted for a moment as if he were trying to puzzle out her words. Then he said, "Just over the hill. I can take you there. Are you ill?"

"No, I'm not ill. If you just point out her house, I can get there myself."

He raised a callused hand to his brow and stared out over the land. "Over there," he said, nodding. "If she's not in the garden, listen for the machines."

"Thank you."

The man nodded again and flicked the reins over the horse's broad back. The cart began to roll.

About twenty minutes later, Corbeau walked up to the house the farmer had indicated. It was a simple stone cottage, but the building, fence, and grounds looked well maintained. A riotous jungle of flowers and herbs sprawled out between the walls and a low, surrounding fence.

On the west side of the building, a woman was transplanting something exotic-looking into a patch of rich, dark earth. A three-legged dog nosed through the undergrowth near her feet. Corbeau's heart began to pound. The woman was kneeling, her back to the road. Dark hair peeked out from beneath her wide-brimmed straw hat. It was long enough to brush her shoulders, now.

What should she say? What could she say? Would Maria Kalderash even want to see her? Sensing her presence, the dog turned. A thin growl began in its throat.

Her back still to Corbeau, Maria put a calming hand on her dog. She stood slowly, stretching as she rose. Country life had been kind to her. Her body had grown softer, and her skin seemed to glow. When she turned, the sun glinted off the lens of the Eye, and she smiled. "Inspector, I was wondering when you'd arrive."

Only a few yards separated the garden from the road. But to Corbeau, the distance seemed interminable.

At last, Maria reached the front gate. She reached down and popped open the latch. "Do come in," she said. A lively spark danced in her natural eye. The dog nuzzled Corbeau's hand with its cold, wet nose. When Maria took Corbeau's other hand in her own, Corbeau thought she might die of relief. "Do come in, Inspector. May I call you Elise? We have a lot to talk about."

—END—

# About the Author

Before trying her hand at fiction, Jess Faraday trained as a linguist and translator. After a number of years in education, and a handful of published translations, she produced her first novel, *The Affair of the Porcelain Dog*. A voracious reader, avid martial artist, and outdoor enthusiast, she enjoys hiking, camping, and cycling.

# Books Available from Bold Strokes Books

**The Left Hand of Justice** by Jess Faraday Mystery. A kidnapped heiress, a heretical cult, a corrupt police chief, and an accused witch. Paris is burning, and the only one who can put out the fire is Detective Inspector Elise Corbeau…whose boss wants her dead. (978-1-60282-863-6)

**Raising Hell: Demonic Gay Erotica** edited by Todd Gregory. *Raising Hell*: hot stories of gay erotica featuring demons. (978-1-60282-768-4)

**Pursued** by Joel Gomez-Dossi. Openly gay college student Jamie Bradford becomes romantically involved with two men at the same time, and his hell begins when one of his boyfriends becomes intent on killing him. (978-1-60282-769-1)

**Promises in Every Star** edited by Todd Gregory. Acclaimed gay male erotica author Todd Gregory's definitive collection of short stories, including both classic and new works. (978-1-60282-787-5)

**Tricks of the Trade: Magical Gay Erotica** edited by Jerry L. Wheeler. Today's hottest erotica writers take you inside the sultry, seductive world of magicians and their tricks-professional and otherwise. (978-1-60282-781-3)

**Straight Boy Roommate** by Kev Troughton. Tom isn't expecting much from his first term at University, but a chance encounter with straight boy Dan catapults him into an extraordinary, wild weekend of sex and self-discovery, which turns his life upside down, and leads him into his first love affair. (978-1-60282-782-0)

**The Jesus Injection** by Eric Andrews-Katz. Murderous statues, demented drag queens, political bombings, ex-gay ministries, espionage, and romance are all in a day's work for a top-secret agent. But the gloves are off when Agent Buck 98 comes up against The Jesus Injection. (978-1-60282-762-2)

**Combustion** by Daniel W. Kelly. Bearish detective Deck Waxer comes to the city of Kremfort Cove to investigate why the hottest men in town are bursting into flames in broad daylight. (978-1-60282-763-9)

**Young Bucks: Novellas of Twenty-Something Lust & Love** edited by Richard Labonte. Four writers still in their twenties-or with their twenties a nearby memory-write about what it's like to be young, on the prowl for sex, or looking to fall in love. (978-1-60282-770-7)

**Night Shadows: Queer Horror** edited by Greg Herren and J.M. Redmann. *Night Shadows* features delightfully wicked stories by some of the biggest names in queer publishing. (978-1-60282-751-6)

**Secret Societies** by William Holden. An outcast hustler, his unlikely "mother," his faithless lovers, and his religious persecutors—all in 1726. (978-1-60282-752-3)

**Wyatt: Doc Holliday's Account of an Intimate Friendship** by Dale Chase. Erotica writer Dale Chase takes the remarkable friendship between Wyatt Earp, upright lawman, and Doc Holliday, Southern gentlemen turned gambler and killer, to an entirely new level: hot! (978-1-60282-755-4)

**The Jetsetters** by David-Matthew Barnes. As rock band the Jetsetters skyrockets from obscurity to superstardom, Justin Holt, a lonely barista, and Diego Delgado, the band's guitarist, fight with everything they have to stay together, despite the chaos and fame. (978-1-60282-745-5)

**Strange Bedfellows** by Rob Byrnes. Partners in life and crime, Grant Lambert and Chase LaMarca are hired to make a politician's compromising photo disappear, but what should be an easy job quickly spins out of control. (978-1-60282-746-2)

**Sweat: Gay Jock Erotica** edited by Todd Gregory. Sizzling tales of smoking-hot sex with the athletic studs everyone fantasizes about. (978-1-60282-669-4)

**The Marrying Kind** by Ken O'Neill. Just when successful wedding planner Adam More decides to protest inequality by quitting the business and boycotting marriage entirely, his only sibling announces her engagement. (978-1-60282-670-0)

**Boys of Summer** edited by Steve Berman. Stories of young love and adventure, when the sky's ceiling is a bright blue marvel, when another boy's laughter at the beach can distract from dull summer jobs. (978-1-60282-663-2)

**Calendar Boys** by Zachary Logan. A man a month will keep you excited year round. (978-1-60282-665-6)

**Buccaneer Island** by J.P. Beausejour. In the rough world of Caribbean piracy, a man is what he makes of himself—or what a stronger man makes of him. (978-1-60282-658-8)

**Twelve O'Clock Tales** by Felice Picano. The fourth collection of short fiction by legendary novelist and memoirist Felice Picano. Thirteen dark tales that will thrill and disturb, discomfort and titillate, enthrall and leave you wondering. (978-1-60282-659-5)

**Words to Die By** by William Holden. Sixteen answers to the question: What causes a mind to curdle? (978-1-60282-653-3)